The Tumble Inn

The Tumble Inn

William Loizeaux

SYRACUSE UNIVERSITY PRESS

First Edition 2014
14 15 16 17 18 19 6 5 4 3 2 1

An earlier version of chapter 6 previously appeared as "Up the Brook," *The Three Quarter Review*, May 2013.

∞ The paper used in this publication meets the minimum requirements of the American National Standard for Information Sciences—Permanence of Paper for Printed Library Materials, ANSI Z39.48-1992.

For a listing of books published and distributed by Syracuse University Press, visit www.SyracuseUniversityPress.syr.edu.

ISBN: 978-0-8156-1042-7 (paper) 978-0-8156-5303-5 (e-book)

Library of Congress Cataloging-in-Publication Data
Loizeaux, William.
The Tumble Inn / William Loizeaux.
pages cm
Summary: "Tired of their high school teaching jobs and discouraged by their failed attempts at conceiving a child, Mark and Fran Finley decide they need a change in their lives. Abruptly, they leave their friends and family in suburban New Jersey to begin anew as innkeepers on a secluded lake in the Adirondack Mountains" — Provided by publisher.
ISBN 978-0-8156-1042-7 (pbk. : alk. paper) — ISBN 978-0-8156-5303-5 (e-book) 1. Married people—Fiction. 2. High school teachers—Fiction. 3. Life change events—Fiction. 4. Taverns (Inns)—Fiction. 5. Clifton (N.J.)—Fiction. 6. Adirondack Mountains Region (N.Y.)—Fiction. 7. Domestic fiction. 8. Psychological fiction. I. Title.
PS3612.O428T86 2014
813'.6—dc23 2014020902

Manufactured in the United States of America

For Beth and Emma

William Loizeaux is the author of short stories, essays, and two memoirs: *The Shooting of Rabbit Wells* and *Anna: A Daughter's Life*, a *New York Times* Notable Book. He has also written two novels for young readers: *Clarence Cochran, A Human Boy* and *Wings*, which received an ASPCA Henry Berg Children's Book Award and was the 2006 Golden Kite Honor Book for Fiction. He lives with his wife, Beth, in Boston, where he is Writer-in-Residence at Boston University.

Acknowledgments

My thanks go out . . .

To The Maryland State Arts Council for its Individual Artist Award, which helped fund this project.

To the staff at Syracuse University Press and Maria Hosmer-Briggs, my copyeditor, for their care.

To the two anonymous readers for the press for their insightful reports.

To Ivy Goodman for reading my manuscript in its early stages, and for her quiet and tactful wisdom.

To Harvey Grossinger for reading, rereading, and re-rereading my manuscript in its middle and later stages, each time offering helpful, detailed commentary, and with apparent good cheer.

To Tim Seldes for his encouragement over the years.

To Jesseca Salky, my agent, for her own multiple readings, and for her advice, faith, and abiding support.

And finally to Beth and Emma for . . . well, I'm afraid there isn't space for all of it here. Let's just leave it at *everything*.

The Tumble Inn

"Mark, look at this," my wife, Fran, said with a little upswing in her voice that I hadn't heard for a while. She leaned toward me and slid the classifieds across the kitchen table. She pointed at one of the advertisements. "Maybe it's us!"

Well, it *wasn't* us, not by a long shot, though the ad did have, even for me, the sort of misty appeal of an alternate life, something you might wonder about in your weaker moments:

Tired of the aggravation?
Want a change?
Want to live and work in a beautiful lakeside setting?

Position open for couple as **Innkeepers** of historic inn on 500 forested acres in the Adirondack Mountains. Experience in small business required. Must be dedicated to highest standards of hospitality and able to perform a variety of tasks, including grounds and facilities maintenance, also managing summer staff. Annual salary. Profit-sharing. Send letter of application to:

Board of Directors
The Tumble Inn
White Birch Lake, NY 12139

"Are you kidding?" I said. "'Managing staff?' 'Facilities maintenance?' We can hardly operate a screwdriver! And what about this 'dedication to hospitality'? We haven't been the most smiley, outgoing people of late."

At the moment, we were in our rat-hole basement apartment, sitting in our busted chairs, courtesy of our landlord, and glancing up toward the hubcaps and trash outside the kitchen window, though Fran was trying to look beyond it all.

"That's exactly why we have to do *something*," she said. "We can't just keep going like this. At least *I* can't!"

"But *innkeepers*? In some godforsaken place without a street address?"

She shrugged her narrow shoulders, but you could feel her revving inside. "Well, it wouldn't hurt to draft a letter," she said.

Now, twenty years later, this still clings to me: Fran, the next evening, banging on our old manual typewriter—this was 1985—the carriage flying back and forth, the little bell dinging at the end of each line. Her red hair is pulled back loosely in a tortoiseshell clip, and her sleeves are pushed up her long arms, like she could plunge into anything. In her eyes is that focused, excited look that seems to make her freckles vibrate. She spins the paper out of the machine. It's "our" letter to the board of directors, she says, and then she reads it aloud.

It began with some dry, factual information. That we lived in Clifton, New Jersey, were both thirty, and married for five years. That she had done the bookkeeping at a local florist before getting her current job as an algebra teacher at nearby Garfield High. That I taught American History and a health class for sophomores in the same school. And that both of us were "attracted by the outdoor life in the mountains," an assertion which was false, though not absolutely, since twice in our illustrious history we'd driven to High Point Park and pitched a tent—each time in the pouring rain.

But all that was only warming up in the bullpen. She read on with even more conviction. Though we were teachers, we were "entrepreneurs at heart." We were "detail-oriented problem solvers." We loved meeting new people. We loved to decorate and cook. We were flexible, with boundless energy. Early risers! I learned that Fran's attraction to seedy thrift shops and flea markets was actually a "passion for antiques." And I learned, to my wonderment, that I liked nothing better than repairing furniture and old machines, particularly appliances. I was "good with my hands." I could fix anything!

She showed me the letter. "So what do you think?"

"Well . . . It's ingenious." And while it bore scant resemblance to our lives just then, I did like that image of ourselves: we were young, resourceful, and optimistic.

"Shall we send it?" she asked, riding the wave of her own enthusiasm.

"All right. But it's crazy," I said. "It won't fool anyone. Nothing will come of it."

As it happened, *everything* would come of that ingenious letter, though we couldn't have known that at the time. Now I wonder if Fran would have written it if she could have foreseen the path it would take us on, and if, in particular, she could have known where that path would lead *her*. For that matter, would I, the next morning, have so casually dropped the stamped envelope into the mailbox at the end of our block, through that little swinging door that you have to pull open, and when it closes of its own accord, it means you can't get the letter back?

Three weeks dragged by. It was the beginning of October. In my history class I was still in the Colonial Period, teaching that favorite high school topic, the Puritans. And in my dreaded health class—the students called it "Germs and Sperms"—I was in the middle of our Human Reproduction unit, trying to encourage those overheated, not-so-Puritan sixteen-year-olds to avoid what Fran and I, for the past year, had been desperately trying to accomplish ourselves. But without any luck. We'd flunked our own Human Reproduction unit. We hadn't conceived a child.

Now we'd finished another school day and another cheery Monday afternoon faculty meeting in which our principal, Mr. Dodson, informed us of additional budget cuts and warned us again to "tighten our belts," though by the looks of his dewlaps and pear-shaped physique, he hadn't tightened his own in years. Anyway, we had crawled back toward our apartment in rush-hour traffic, avoided the broken beer bottles on the sidewalk, opened the three locks on our door, and walked in as I kicked aside the scattered bills on the peeling linoleum beneath our mail slot.

This was one of those "Red Letter Days," as we called them, in the middle of Fran's cycle, which she'd starred on our calendar with a red Sharpie, a late afternoon when we dutifully dropped our book bags, went to our bedroom, pulled down the shade, and pulled back the covers. Trying to play Master of Ceremonies, I lit a candle, set it on top of my bureau, and brought in two glasses of our usual cheap white wine. Sliding into our sheets, we did those things that we'd always done: Fran unclasping the tortoise-shell clip, the slow unbuttoning, unbuckling, unzipping, the two tiny hooks on the back of her bra, the slipping off of pants and underwear, the entwining of legs, the smells of hair and sweat, the building rhythm, our bodies, as familiar to one another as to ourselves, warming to the moment. . . .

Until, on the edge of the moment itself, something involuntary, like a cold shiver, ran through Fran's body and then mine. We stopped. Our hearts weren't in it, and our flesh swiftly followed, everything collapsing and cooling.

"We're pathetic!" Fran said. "It's no use." She could have been speaking for me as well, and we turned away from each other. As if to reassure ourselves, we touched hands under the sheets, though it didn't feel all that reassuring.

"I'm scared," Fran said with tears at her temples in the wavering light. She was staring at the ceiling like she might see something there. "Mark, what's happening to us?"

The next afternoon when we came home from school, I picked up that pile of bills, which had grown bigger behind the door. One of the envelopes stuck out: it looked like a small wedding announcement or a birthday invitation for a kid. It had no return address, the post mark was illegible, and the writing on it, in the dark blue ink of a fountain pen, was either jaggedly aggressive or very shaky. It was hard to tell.

In the kitchen, Fran opened the envelope, unfolded the note, read it to herself, then looked at me, wide-eyed, with such brimming wonder and satisfaction—a little too much satisfaction, in fact. "You stand corrected!" she announced, and handed me the note.

Oct. 5, 1985

Dear Mr. and Mrs. Finley,

We are interested in your application, and we will be interviewing finalists for the position of innkeeper on Saturday, Oct. 19. On that date, could you join the board of directors at the Tumble Inn, so we might get to know each other better? Please call 518-548-9351 to make a reservation and an appointment. Of course, we will provide for your room and board during your stay. We look forward to meeting you.

Sincerely,

Silas Worthington Dunning, Jr., Esq., Chair, Board of Directors

After this, came a "P.S." with directions to the inn, which, among other curious things, involved a right turn near a general store, a three-mile drive on an unmarked dirt road, a hairpin turn, then another right "at the fork with the stand of birches," and finally a sharp left into a gravel driveway. "Mind the bump," it said, "when turning in."

But that was it. The other side of the note was blank. There was nothing more about the job itself, its terms and responsibilities. Nor was there anything remotely informative about the inn. No brochures, pictures, no schedule of rates. How big was it? How many rooms? What sort of clientele did it have? What kind of operation was this, anyway?

Suspicion flickered up in my mind. Maybe *we* were being fooled. Who on earth would have a name like Silas Worthington Dunning, Jr., Esq.? Maybe there was no such person. Maybe no lake. No inn.

I was about to take this up with Fran, but she'd run out to our ancient Volkswagen van and had already come back with a road map of New York State, and was unfolding it on the table. She flattened it out with her palms. She leaned over it like a field commander. Straight up the Thruway she went with her finger, then onto Route 30 and west on Route 8. Now she followed a thin, gray, squiggly line until the trail of paved roads ran out. Then her finger wandered over areas without any towns, just rivers and peaks with elevations. Eventually, it came to a stop. She peered more closely. And there, smaller but shaped almost like her own pinky, was a narrow finger, a sky-blue body of water, unlabeled, squeezed between ridges and pointing northwest.

"Bingo!" she said.

"How do you know?"

"Quick, let's make the reservation, before all the rooms are taken!" Fran had a way of doing this sometimes, pushing us forward faster than I could dig in my heels.

Half expecting a message saying, "This number has been disconnected," I dialed the number on the note. I let it ring six, seven, ten times. Obviously, it was a bogus number, some pay phone ringing in an empty parking lot.

Then a bright female voice said, "Tumble Inn. May I help you?"

I hauled my mind away from the empty parking lot and asked if Silas Worthington Dunning, Jr. was available. I couldn't say the "esquire" part.

"I'm afraid he's downstate," the voice said. "He won't be up until next weekend. Can I take a message?"

I told her that I was calling about next weekend. My wife and I had received a note inviting us for an interview.

"Then you must be Mr. Finley!" she said. "I've heard so much about you! I'm Abby, Mr. Dunning's grandniece. I'm helping hold down the fort up here. We've kept room six open for you and your wife. I think you'll like it. It looks over the lake!"

I said that sounded nice, but I was wondering if I might speak with someone about the job. I was fuzzy on the details.

She said, "Oh, then you'll have to talk with Mr. Dunning," and she gave me a phone number with an area code in New York City. "So shall we book you for Friday night? There's a breakfast appointment available for Saturday morning at eight o'clock, bright and early."

I covered the receiver with my hand and asked Fran about this.

"Definitely!" she said. "Take it! We can cut out of school on Friday after lunch and get up there for dinner!"

Right then, it didn't occur to me just how we both might "cut out of school," dropping our afternoon classes, without getting ourselves good and fired. Fran's eyes just said it would happen, and if it didn't—or once we'd come to our senses about this—I figured we could always cancel the reservation. So I went ahead and made it, another one of those small decisions that look a bit larger in retrospect.

Next I called Mr. Dunning, and again was mildly surprised to hear a voice come on the line. But it wasn't his. Mr. Dunning, the voice said, was "indisposed" at the moment. I was speaking with a Mr. Blake, his "associate," at what I assumed was a place of business.

Could Mr. Dunning call back? I asked. Or could I call him at a more convenient time?

"Perhaps I can be of help," Mr. Blake said with a kind of amiable insistence. "On most matters, we work together."

I asked if he knew anything about a place called the Tumble Inn.

"Of course!" He said he was on the board of directors.

So I told him who I was, and he was happy to fill me in on what he called "the basics." The inn, built in the 1890s on the north end of White

Birch Lake, was "quaint and cozy," just eight guest rooms, all on the second floor. It was owned by a group of ten families from Westchester who long ago had formed a company, of which Mr. Dunning was now the president and chairman of the board, and he, Mr. Blake, was the treasurer. For a token annual fee, the company leased the inn to the innkeepers, who pretty much had free reign in running the day-to-day operation. They would set the rates, hire and supervise a small, usually seasonal staff, and serve breakfast and dinner to the guests, most of whom were the many relatives, friends, and acquaintances of the founding families. Summers were always busy at the inn and winters occasionally busy on weekends with clubs or skiing groups. In March, April, May, September, October, and November, it was practically empty. Weeks and weeks could go by without any guests. The inn *was* open to members of the public, he said, and it wasn't unusual for a few to venture into the driveway if they were exploring the back roads.

I asked why the job had opened, and he said that the previous innkeepers, a couple that had worked there for thirty years, had decided to retire to Florida. Then I asked about the salary that was unspecified in the newspaper ad, and he was pleased to report that it had been raised to $7,000, which was over and above the innkeepers' free living quarters and their fifty percent of the business profits. The job would begin on January first. The contract would be for a year and, if things went satisfactorily, was renewable by approval of the board.

As he spoke, I took notes, and when I'd finished on the phone, Fran and I looked them over. The salary, I said, was piddling, the profits unpredictable. We wouldn't be contributing to our pensions. Financially speaking, it looked chancy. "And that's to say nothing of uprooting from family and friends, from everything we know."

"Come on! When *would* you take a chance? When *would* you make a big change?" Fran was quick to say. "What more do you want? Free room and board. A guaranteed income with the possibility of more. No monthly rent."

"No slimy landlord," I acknowledged.

"Family and friends can always visit," she said. "And a lake! Imagine. Canoes. Woods. Mountain air. Space for a kid to run around!"

Looking back, I can still feel how we were carried away, how things gathered such heady momentum, while at the same time, it amazes me that we were even having this conversation and taking ourselves seriously. It was as if, for a time, we'd forgotten who we'd been, that our lives had seemed so stuck. It was as if we'd forgotten that we hadn't yet been interviewed, that we hadn't yet seen this inn, not even a photo, and that we weren't remotely qualified for the job. No one, perhaps, had been fooling us. Instead, it was more like we were fooling ourselves, imagining that in a whole different place we could start anew.

To teach high school kids, you have to know your stuff, but to communicate what you know deeply into their oily pores, it helps if some part of you, no matter how old you are, still loves the impulsive energy and nervy excitement of teenagers. Fran, I think, truly felt that, at least in our early years at Garfield. In the classroom, she was all heat and inspiration, scratching new equations on the board with one hand, while erasing old ones with the other. When she gave her students a word problem, say on ratios and proportions, she wouldn't follow the math text, asking them to compute the percentage of medals won by such-and-such country in the most recent Olympics. Instead, she'd toss the book aside, and I mean literally *toss* it aside. Off the top of her head, she'd ask how fast you'd have to drive your girlfriend in your bucket-seated, mag-wheeled Firebird between exits five and three on the Parkway, that is, if you'd been averaging seventy miles per hour between all the other exits, and had gotten on the Parkway at 3:00 a.m., and you were just dying to get to Wildwood beach at exactly 5:58, when you'd both roll up in a blanket, tight as sardines, and watch the sun rise over the water, among other amusing activities. That was Fran.

Need I say that I was a different sort of teacher? Desperately, I tried to be clear and logical in the chaos of high school life. On the board, I'd neatly outline in Roman numeral headings and alphabetized subheadings the causes and effects of, say, The Great Awakening, which promptly put the class to sleep.

Because proximity would have invited even more comparisons of Fran and me, it was probably good, certainly for me, that we worked in distant parts of the school. Math/Science was in the north wing, and Social Studies/Language in the west, "like the setting sun," Fran said, and not without some accuracy. On Fridays, however, she and I had lunch duty together—our job was to keep the food fights to a minimum—and it was on the Friday following my conversations with Abby and Mr. Blake that our esteemed principal, Mr. Dodson, strode into the cafeteria with an aggrieved look on his fleshy face. His stomach, as always, hung over his belt. His sport coat didn't button around his middle. His arms stuck out penguin-like from his body, and he walked with the brisk and splay-footed self-importance of certain administrators who enjoy what little power they have. He came right up to us and told us to follow him. "You can leave your lunches where they are."

In his office, Mr. Dodson closed the door, said, "Sit down" in his most serious voice, and announced that he had some bad news. Ms. Farrell, his secretary, had just gotten a call from the hospital. Fran's mother, he regretted to inform us, had suddenly taken ill and had been rushed to the emergency room in grave condition. Of course, this turn of events had put him in "a difficult situation." No substitute teachers were immediately available, so he'd have to "twist some arms" to cover our classes. Still, in what we were to understand was an outpouring of magnanimity, he allowed that he'd "bend over backwards" and let us take the afternoon off so that we could be with Fran's mother.

We thanked him profusely, saying that his generosity was particularly appreciated just then, as Fran's father was away on business. We walked out of his office and down the hall to get our jackets from our lockers. Already the news had gotten out. Bob Lang, a chemistry teacher we barely knew, paused to say, "I'm very sorry." We walked down the stairs, holding tight to the railing and keeping our eyes straight forward. Down another hallway, we came to the door that led to the parking lot. I unlocked it—the school was a so-called "drug-free zone," a proud prison oasis. Then, squinting, we were out in the warm, open air, the sun skating on windshields.

It was all a brilliant ruse of course, mostly of Fran's devising. She had arranged for a friend to call the school and report the grave illness of her mother, who in fact at that moment was altogether healthy, eating little cucumber sandwiches with her bridge group in Montclair. So as Fran and I moved purposefully to our van, we still didn't speak, nor did we dare look at one another. Anyone could have been watching us through the school windows, and we could have blown it all right then.

We got in and put on our seatbelts. Our suitcases were beneath a towel in the back seat, the map and note from Mr. Dunning folded in the glove box. I carefully drove out of the lot, switched on the turn signal, and stopped for a whole beat at the intersection. I turned right onto Outwater Lane, and when we were around the corner, out of view of all those windows, I caught Fran's eye or she caught mine, and for a second we just shook our heads, marveling that we were doing this. Then, like our students on the last day of school, we exploded, whooping, the radio blaring, and me whipping through the gears like a pro, shooting that rusted, one-lung van out of town. Out of state. Heading north.

Long ago, the Dutch East India Company had an interesting idea. When things at home are getting a little cloying, unprofitable, or boring, try something new. Liven things up by hiring an explorer to cross the Atlantic and search the American coastline for the Northwest Passage to Asia. In 1609, Henry Hudson, with twenty brave souls on his ship, the *Half Moon*, thought that he had found it: a wide, navigable river, bounded by palisades and shimmering perhaps with exotic oriental light. Instead of in China, however, this Northwest Passage ended up in Albany. But no matter. It was still the New World. Lots of possibilities. And like the great explorer, Fran and I, straining to see beyond every bend, now wound our way up the Hudson Valley, though in a different, more fragile vessel and by a slightly more circuitous route.

Past Albany, we headed due west on the Thruway and followed the Mohawk River, another trail of bold pioneers. At Amsterdam, an old, ramshackle factory town, we turned north again, onto Route 30. With Fran tracking our every move on the map, we went through small, early nineteenth-century villages with streets lined with maples that glowed yellow and gold. In only three or four hours, it seemed, we'd moved forward from late summer to mid fall, as well as backward into history. Along the Sacandaga River, we hit our first big stands of pines. Then we left the river and started climbing for real. There, up ahead, were the mountains, rounded like owls' heads. Except for the occasional lonely restaurant or motel, the forest was uninterrupted. At a town called Speculator, we turned onto Route 8, and ten miles later we passed the general store mentioned in the note, a swaybacked, two-story frame house with a single Sinclair gas pump in the gravel and a battered sign hanging cockeyed from the porch gutter:

ORMA'S
Worms, Ammo, Wood, Gas, Food, Anything
Potluck every other Fri Nite

We parked and, as we went in, a couple of bells jingled on the door, and then beneath the speckled fly paper that twisted down from the tin ceiling, a stocky woman emerged from behind a wood-burning stove. She moved in the way that people often do up here, in a low gear that is slow but inevitable, as if conserving energy in a place where the winters are cold and long.

She smiled and lumbered in behind the long counter where there was a cash register and behind that, rough wooden shelves stuffed with matches, compasses, soap, wool socks, long johns, toilet paper, Pepto-Bismol, mousetraps, Sterno, jackknives, and Jack Daniels—such necessities being Orma's stock-in-trade.

The woman, who turned out to be Orma, asked if she could help us. She wore thick glasses, a white apron, had her hair pinned up, a nub of pencil behind one ear, and while I had the sense that she was older than we were, you couldn't guess her age. One of her arms ended in a calloused stump at her elbow.

"We'd like some gas," I said. "Ten dollars." I opened my wallet, but she shook her head and said, "Pay *after* you've pumped."

I went out and put gas in the car, watching the little numbers go around. In the time that I fueled up and washed the windshield, a single vehicle, a mud-splashed truck, rattled by. I looked at my watch: rush hour.

Back inside, Fran and Orma were making small talk. I paid Orma my ten dollars. Then out of the blue, she said, "You're not the new innkeepers, are you?"

Fran and I glanced at each other. "No," Fran said, "but we'd like to be. We're being interviewed tomorrow."

Orma looked at us, up and down, and what she saw must have pained her. She sighed, and with her tongue made a clicking sound. "Want a piece of advice?" she asked me.

I didn't have a chance to answer.

"Your shoes." She was referring to my loafers, the ones I always wore to school. "Have you got anything else in the car?"

I shook my head.

"What size?"

I told her nine, sometimes nine-and-a-half.

She went to the back of the store through a curtained doorway beside a Coke machine and returned with a pair of beat-up leather work boots, which she carried in her good arm. She sat me down on a wooden crate, and had me try them on right there and then, handing me a pair of wool socks—"no charge"—to put over my own cotton ones. As I laced the boots, she turned her attention to Fran, who was in her jeans and a sweater she'd put on in the car. "I guess you'll be all right," Orma said. Then, giving Fran a look that didn't exactly fill me with confidence: "It's your husband who's the challenge."

With the extra socks, the boots fit.

"Wear those at the interview," Orma said in her no-nonsense way. "They'll be wanting a man in boots."

We thanked her and went to the door, me carrying my loafers, and both of us a little bewildered by the interest an utter stranger had taken in us. Orma waved us off with her stump. She was the first person we'd met here. We'd talked for five minutes, ten at the most, and already she must have figured us out. We were still a young couple, but feeling older, with jobs we didn't like, an uncertain future, no child to give it form, and without enough experience yet to know the difference between a lark and a big risk. People just don't come up here looking for work in October, with winter coming on, unless they've got as much trouble as hope and have thrown caution to the wind.

Back in the car, we pulled away from the gas pump, and soon, near a small shelter for a school bus stop, I turned onto the dirt road. I drove slowly, sometimes even in first gear, no faster than a runner might jog. The surface was practically corrugated, a washboard, with stones the size of baseballs that rattled against the underbody. Aside from the road itself, a rickety plank bridge was the only sign of human activity. I *did* see what looked like a path into the woods, a certain winding disturbance in the leaves, but so thin and evanescent—it must have been a deer trail.

Over the last few miles, Fran and I didn't speak. While her foot drummed nervously on the floor mat, we just watched the woods coming at us, drawing us in, and then closing up quickly behind us. As we climbed, we tunneled deeper and deeper into the forest, into mixed growth with evergreens now, into tamaracks, spruces, balsams, and towering white pines, none of which we could have named right then, though I think we felt how they changed and darkened, the thickening textures and resinous smells, and the way the high limbs curtained off the sky.

I drove slower and slower on account of the incline, as well as a renewed hesitancy on my part. I turned on the headlights. We came to the hairpin turn, where we seemed to be heading back toward New Jersey, which struck me as a not altogether unreasonable idea. But at the fork with the white-barked birch trees dead ahead, I veered right, and soon grass sprang up between the tracks, and a limb brushed the van's antenna. A simple wooden sign saying "Rooms & Meals" appeared in my lights.

"We're here," Fran said, and I turned into the driveway. But too fast. I didn't sufficiently "mind the bump," a huge pine root that sent us reeling, the suitcases flying, the glove box slamming open and all its contents pouring out. Like everyone's first trip to the inn, ours ended with a jolt. Maybe that's why it's called "The Tumble Inn."

So we'd arrived. It was dusk. And what we saw next, as I inched the car toward the small gravel parking lot, was very much like what I see now, when I return, say, from Stephenson's Lumber and Hardware, and ease the pickup down the driveway. The trees pull back. The sky opens. Straight ahead the lawn fans across the wide knoll, then gently descends for about fifty yards, changing into the field that I sickle down twice a year, which in turn gives way to the long swath of sandy beach that I rake each spring and have raked again this fall. Only a few picnic tables and the green-shingled boathouse with the long, attached dock interrupt the beach. Beyond that, the lake spreads out like an open palm, filled with evening light. It's a mile wide and six long, with a small, wooded island about a half mile out there. Then beyond the water, the dark hills unfurl to the south and west, ridge after ridge, each a little lighter than the one before, and the mountain rises to the east. On certain evenings at dusk, especially in the violet light of September and October, those hills give me a pang. They look like the silhouettes of reclining bodies: the shape, for instance, of a sleeping girl's shoulders, or the long, flowing slope of a woman's back, thighs, and calves.

This is not the most spectacular view you'll ever see. There are higher vantage points, bigger lakes, and many more aspiring, rock-faced mountains, especially among the "High Peaks" up north. But if I had to choose a view to live out my days with, this would be the one. Usually it's serene. The water is flat, the land smoothed and furred with trees. The big geological events, the shifting of plates and the upheaval of mountains, are all eons old. Everything cataclysmic has already happened, and this is the land that's left. Everything is in its accustomed place. Everything, it seems, is settled.

From the back floor of the van, Fran and I retrieved our suitcases, then walked slightly uphill and past a swing set, where the inn came into view at the top of a knoll, and I felt Fran put her arm through the crook of mine. The inn did, in fact, appear quaint and cozy: a red tin roof, three dormers, two picture windows on the bottom floor, and a forest-green wraparound porch, all looking across a wide lawn and out toward the lake. Smoke curled from one of the chimneys, and a table lamp, framed by parted curtains, glowed in the middle dormer window. The sign beside the porch door said, "Office. Please come in." We knocked once, then again, and since no one seemed to have heard us, we stepped inside.

The air smelled faintly of cedar. We heard a fire crackling. On the wall, a couple of plaid lumberjack coats hung on pegs. To the right, we saw the office behind a polished wood reception desk, along with the open guest book, a ballpoint pen on a beaded chain, and the little silver bell to ring for service. We rang the bell a few times, but no one came. So what else to do? We walked down the short entrance hall, and called, "Hello? Hello? Anybody home?"

We called up the stairs. We peered into a large living room where a fire blazed in a stone hearth decorated above the mantelpiece with crossed snowshoes. An unfinished jigsaw puzzle lay on a card table beneath a standing lamp. There were bulky sofas, sagging bookcases, frayed throw rugs, empty rush-seated chairs, and on the walls hung tilted black-and-white landscape photographs in birch-bark frames. "It's lovely," Fran said, for some reason in a whisper. And she was right. It all had a warm, informal, though not quite disheveled, feel.

We heard steps on the porch stairs, feet stomping on the mat, and the door opening and closing. Soon a woman in jeans, a heavy sweatshirt, and hiking boots stood in the living room doorway. She looked to be in her late twenties, thick-boned, rugged, with a broad, open face, a kind smile, a pony tail, and in her arms she carried a load of split logs. "You must be the Finleys!" she said in that same bright voice that I'd heard a few days before on the phone.

"And you must be Abby," I said.

When she'd set the wood on the hearth and taken off her gloves, we all shook hands. Then she took our suitcases and led us upstairs. The floorboards creaked with every step, and the hallway tilted to the left. We passed open doorways, where we caught glimpses of iron bed frames, quilts, or a washstand with folded towels on top.

Our own room, #6, was charming. It was the dormer room at the end of the hall, the biggest, with sprigged wallpaper, two full dressers, and a queen-size four-poster bed with a crocheted canopy above it. Beginning that evening, Fran and I would jokingly call it the "Honeymoon Suite," though it wasn't really a suite at all, and we were some distance now from our official honeymooning days.

We ate dinner downstairs at the table for two in the dining room corner beneath the framed Winslow Homer prints. Four large, oval oak tables filled the rest of the room, most with place settings for eight or ten, though we were the only guests there. Abby, in an apron, lit a candle between us, then served baked chicken, rice, and steamed broccoli that drooped on our forks. When she came out of the kitchen to see how everything was, we said, "Delicious!" and finally Fran asked her, "So where *is* everyone, I mean the board of directors? We're still having our interview tomorrow morning, aren't we?"

"Oh," Abby said, "I should have explained. On their way up here, they all meet for dinner in Albany. They'll arrive later tonight, no telling when." She didn't mention, nor did we ask about, when the other finalists for the job would arrive.

After apple pie for dessert, Fran and I put on our jackets and walked out on the lawn. Along the distant shore, a few specks of light glimmered and were doubled on the surface of the lake. There was a crescent moon, the sky like tarnished pewter above the dark hills. No wind. A mist had fallen, and on the grass it had turned into glistening frost. We stayed close, each with an arm around the other, to keep ourselves a little warmer.

Whatever we said then must have been unremarkable. I can't remember a word of it now. What I do remember were those specks of light, the sky, the hills, the frost, and a certain thawing of my resistance to things. *What would it be like to live here?* Not unrelated to this was the feel of Fran's sharp hip through her clothing and the softness below her ribs. Just as I am not a "handsome" man in the way you usually think of that term, Fran was not a "gorgeous" nor a "beautiful" woman. She was lean and angular. Her body made you think of its bones. But she was pretty, and she was strong in a taut, long-muscled way that never ceased to surprise me. Set with a purpose, she could outlast just about anything. The things she grasped she hated to give up, and somehow, amazingly, I was one of them. I still am.

Sometime in the middle of that night, I awoke hearing noises. The *ker-thunk, ker-thunk* of cars bottoming out, and the sputter of engines turning off. Doors opening and closing. Trunks too. Then feet scuffing on gravel. I heard voices laughing, some complaining: "This damn hill gets steeper each year!" Now the porch door banged. Then steps on the stairs and steps on the floorboards outside our door. Something or someone bumped against a wall, probably where the hall really tilts. Then more laughter, though muffled. They—the board members, I presumed—were trying to be quiet, which of course made everything seem louder. There was grunting and the clatter of luggage. The tingle of coat hangers in closets. Water ran, toilets whooshed, and someone gargled. Next there was a lot of coughing and clearing of throats, followed by hushed "Goodnight"s. Eventually, though, it all died down, leaving only Fran's feathery breath beside me, and from the woods, the faint gurgle of a brook as it wound toward the lake.

When we awoke at dawn, it was quiet, as if I had dreamed all those noises. But when, in our robes, we tiptoed down the hall, all the other doors were closed, and from behind them came the sounds of snoring. We dressed in sweaters, jackets, and jeans, Fran in sneakers and me in my hand-me-down boots. We were getting the feel of things here. As quietly as possible, we went downstairs, where breakfast would be served in forty-five minutes. In the living room, the fire was out, the sofas empty, so we walked outside onto the porch. We sat on rocking chairs, hands thrust into pockets, as the sun edged over the side of the mountain.

Soon Abby came out with mugs of strong coffee. "Don't worry. You'll be great," she said, smiling, and at exactly eight o'clock, she rang a bell on the corner post, and we went inside to the dining room. At one of the oval tables, at all the ten place settings save for ours, the members of the board were comfortably ensconced, as though they'd sat in those exact places for years. Most of them appeared to be in their sixties or seventies. The women, in turtlenecks or cardigans, gave the impression of once being nurses or teachers, still alert, engaged, still in the habit of putting themselves to productive, if less strenuous, use. And the men, in loose shirts and corduroy or khaki pants, had that easy-going look of successful businessmen who'd recently retired. One man, to be honest, looked downright youthful in this company, sharp and spry in his mid-forties, wearing those half-glasses that you often see on lawyers and librarians. This turned out to be Mr. Blake, the treasurer, who was giving his attention to the silent man at the head of the table, an ancient patriarch with long, fleshy ears and a tremor that made his string tie twitch.

Fran's eyes and mine met for an instant. Was this old guy okay? *Who is he?*

He turned out to be Silas Worthington Dunning, Jr., Esq., President and Chair of the Board. His actual chair, the one he was slumped into, was of the wheeled variety.

Standing, Mr. Blake greeted us, shook our hands, and we took our seats. With her shoulders thrown back and face beaming toward them, Fran gave me a little nudge with her elbow, as if to say, *Look alive!*

In a friendly voice, Mr. Blake, who seemed to be speaking for Mr. Dunning as well, introduced himself and the other members of the board. Across the table sat Mrs. Boatwright—"Call me Beverly"—the large-chested, cheerful head of the Housekeeping Committee. Next to her sat Ted Irving, who nodded his sleek, white head of hair, and his industrious wife, Kay, who was leaning back, knitting a scarf, the needles clicking like clockwork. To our left was the Secretary, Ms. Fringe, already scribbling in her notebook. Then came Eleanor Cooledge, with her glasses hanging on a cord around her neck. And finally, Dan Norman, with his jutting, lantern jaw, who reached across the table to vigorously shake our hands. "So pleased to meet you!" He was head of the Grounds Committee.

Then Fran and I introduced ourselves, and, as the bowl of fruit cocktail went around, we all chatted about the glorious fall weather. Some of the board members talked about their children and grandchildren. They asked where we'd grown up (both of us in New Jersey suburbs) and where we'd gone to college (we'd met at Rutgers) and what it was like teaching sophomores in high school. "A handful," Fran said, to laughter.

Through all this, they were kind and encouraging in the way of aunts and uncles, and we tried to be charming and helpful, like the innkeepers we thought we wanted to be. At one point, Fran got up, took the coffee pot, and to expressions like "Thank you dear, just a splash," she refilled mugs all around.

After the pancakes, though, things got more serious. We were beginning the real interview now, as Mr. Blake began with a question. He wanted to know why we'd come all the way up here, when we had good jobs down below.

Fran answered this smartly, saying that we were "ready for a new challenge," and she couldn't think of a job that better fit our personalities, talents, and priorities than being innkeepers here. Beginning our thirties now, we were "anxious to put down roots" and live in a quieter, cleaner, healthier place, where at night you can see the stars. She didn't mention that we wanted to raise a family, and Mr. Blake didn't ask about it directly, though I've often wondered if he and the others could see it in our faces, and if they liked what we thought we were hiding.

Instead, Dan Norman asked about our business experience and how that might be applied to our operation of the inn. Again Fran leaped right in, telling them that when she had worked at Monroe's Florist she had been responsible for keeping all revenue, inventory, and expense accounts, including taxes, insurance, and payroll. Then for some minutes, she and Mr. Blake had an animated discussion about "income projections," "occupancy rates," and "cash flow," a discussion that I was happy to avoid, though I could feel my time coming.

I especially felt it when Mr. Blake pulled our application letter from his breast pocket and, using his pen as a pointer, began to silently review it. He peered at me over the top of his half-glasses. "So, I understand you're quite the handyman."

"Well . . ." But that was all I could say.

"Now, don't be modest," he said, passing the fruit around again. "It says here that you're a sort of jack-of-all-trades, a troubleshooter, and as you might imagine, that's the most important thing around here. What with the winter weather and the hard summer use, it isn't easy to keep on top of things. The water system, the septic, the electric, the boiler, the roof, the boathouse, the dock, the mowers, the tractor—you name it. If it isn't one thing, it's another. An innkeeper here is also a repairman. You have to think fast, patch and mend, fix all kinds of things."

I still couldn't say very much, so I just said, "Yes sir."

Then he said, "So let me ask you a question. Say you have the inn full of guests. Say it's a late-summer weekend, the kitchen's going full blast, you've just served dinner, it's getting dark outside, and all at once a thunderstorm comes over the mountains and the electricity all goes out. That means no lights, no refrigeration. The well won't pump, so no toilets, showers, or baths. Mind you, we have a generator, but it's small, only three thousand watts. So how would you handle that situation? What steps might you take?"

I now know just what I'd do. I've done it any number of times. I'd tell the guests we've been through this before. I'd pass out flashlights. I'd say let's think of this as camping out. This is, after all, the Adirondacks. Then I'd go out to the garage and get the generator going. Soon I could power up a couple of circuits, the kitchen and part of the dining room. Next, I'd turn off the valve at the well and open the one from the old spring house in the woods, so we'd have enough pressure to run the toilets. Then on the gas range, I'd start boiling water for drinking. In this way, we'd limp along, jerry-rigging, shutting circuits off and turning others on, until we'd make it through to the morning.

That's how I'd answer Mr. Blake today, but at the time I drew a blank. I wasn't even sure what a generator was, and the only words that finally came to me were, "Well, I guess we'd just make do."

At this, some of the board members nodded with relief and approval. Had I hit on the right answer?

But Mr. Blake's eyebrows squinched together, and his mouth went small, as with something unexpectedly distasteful. He wasn't satisfied with my reply, and he pressed on. "Yes, but how *exactly* might you 'make do'? How would you work around the problem?"

Now I couldn't say a word. Nor did anyone else. In the long, sweating silence, I must have looked like a deer caught in headlights. Kay Irving paused in her knitting. She leaned forward to join the others, and I felt the full force of the board's disappointment, their suddenly doubtful faces. They'd found me out. I was a fraud. The boots I was wearing weren't mine. Everything was falling apart, and again I felt Fran's sharp elbow.

"Well . . . ?" Mr. Blake said at last.

Still, I couldn't say anything.

And then it happened. Though your decisions do shape your life, it's luck or pure, out-of-the-blue accident that radically changes it—for better or for worse.

As the faces around the table bore into me, one of them turned pale and then immediately blue with a kind of frantic, soundless gasping. It was Mr. Dunning. He clutched his throat, his string tie thrashing. Everyone turned to him, horrified, and someone cried, "Oh my God!"

Maybe because I'd been the first to see him, or more likely because I was already on the verge of flight, I was the first out of my seat. I went right to him and—this was extraordinary—I knew what to do! How many times, using the drawing on page sixty-six of our text, had I described it to my students in Health, during our Emergency First Aid unit? The Heimlich maneuver. From behind and grasping him under his arms, I hauled Mr. Dunning, like a sack of potatoes, straight out of his wheelchair. Holding him up with his back against me, I regrasped around his middle, my hands locked in double fists below his solar plexus. With all my might, I pulled sharply up and in, seeming to squeeze his body in half. There was an instant of perilous silence, everyone cringing, as when you've pumped a balloon to almost bursting. Then from his throat, came a popping sound, like a cork from a bottle. Something the size of a kid's marble shot out of his mouth, arched gracefully through the air, and landed beside the potted chrysanthemum in the middle of the table.

It was a grape, a little green grape, perfectly round and whole. It had come from the fruit cocktail that Mr. Dunning had evidently taken a liking to.

I released my grip, returned Mr. Dunning to his wheelchair, where he slumped and shook, but slowly came back to life, regaining his breath and color.

Suddenly, I was a small celebrity! Suddenly, I *was* a repairman! Dan Norman was shaking, then shaking my hand again. Beverly Boatwright crushed me into her amplitude, crying, "Oh, you're a life saver!" Fran squeezed my arm until it hurt and whispered in my ear, "You did it!" And then Mr. Blake, who was kneeling beside the wheelchair, patting Mr. Dunning's wrist, looked up and asked, "What can we do to thank you?"

Fran and I glanced at each other, and Mr. Blake, who saw our glance, seemed to understand what he could do. He announced that this was a good time to end the interview. He asked us to wait in the living room. Apparently, there were no other pressing appointments, and we saw no other interviewees. Perhaps others had been interviewed during the previous weekend, or perhaps no others had been interviewed at all. In any case, Fran and I, too excited to sit, stood next to the picture window, where the morning now had come in full, and the lake stretched out, a deeper blue than the sky.

Soon Mr. Blake asked us to come back in. As we sat again with the board of directors, everyone hushed. . . . And then Mr. Dunning *stood*! Joint by joint, he unfolded himself, rising from his wheelchair, as with his last ounce of strength. Then for the first time, we heard him speak. In a wispy, quavering, but audible voice, he said, "Let's welcome our new innkeepers."

After our interview with the board of directors, Fran and I stayed an extra half day at the inn, so that Abby and Mr. Blake could show us around, while we asked questions and tried to look as intelligent as possible before signing the contract that afternoon. That's how fast it happened. To wait and think about it would have been much too reasonable. Sometimes, against all your better judgment, you just do these things, especially if someone like Fran has a hand in it.

"What's to think about?" she'd asked, laying her hand very gently on the back of mine and fixing me with her hazel eyes that at once seemed hard and warm. We were eating lunch, just she and I, again at the table for two in the inn's dining room. "Mark, this is our chance! It's for *both* of us. You won't have to teach the Puritans anymore. No more faculty meetings. No more food fights. No more detention duty in a room full of adolescent psychopaths. No more Mr. Dodson!"

How at the moment could I have argued with that? "Okay," I'd said, and I'd turned over my hand so I could hold hers.

As the contract provided, we'd start on January first, and as Mr. Blake suggested, we all thought it wise for Abby to continue for at least a month beyond that, overlapping with us. She could help us learn the ropes.

Back home in New Jersey the next week, we gave notice to our landlord. We informed our families, friends, and an enraged Mr. Dodson, who threatened legal action, but would eventually sign our release.

"What, are you out of your minds?" That was the immediate and not encouraging response of our friend and colleague, Howie Sanders, an English teacher, when we told him our news in the school parking lot on the following Tuesday. Through his wire-rim glasses that were always askew, he looked at me with his amused and incredulous eyes, the way he'd sometimes look when we'd exchange what we called "student bloopers," those amazing locutions that turned up on exams and papers. "Unicamel" for "unicameral." "Pre-Madonna" for "prima donna," as in this topic sentence he once showed me: "Cleopatra was a real Pre-Madonna."

Howie was hired the same year we were, fresh out of Montclair State. Recently jilted by Maria Cuervo, Garfield's Spanish teacher and another of Howie's "only" true loves, he lived alone in his own rat-hole apartment in Passaic. He had the same complaints as we did about surly, unmotivated students. Over beers at our kitchen table, the three of us had laughed and cried through our first year when we all learned that teaching high school had less to do with inspiring young minds than slogging from one day to the next.

Now Howie's look was a little more imploring. "You're not really leaving? You're kidding about this innkeeping deal, right?"

I stared at the white line between our parking spaces. No, I said, we weren't kidding.

Then—vintage Howie—he let us have it. "That's the stupidest idea I've ever heard! Twenty years ago, the hippies tried this, headed north to cows, goats, and pastures. Back to nature. They got stoned, got poor, got herpes and gonorrhea, came back, got shaved, got dressed up, and got into . . . advertising. Now *you* want to try the same career path?!"

"It's not some hippie farm or a commune!" Fran shot back, matching him blow for blow. "It's a perfectly respectable *inn*!"

Then Howie's voice changed again and he shook his head sadly. "I thought we were all in this together here."

During the following weeks, Fran and I managed to get our engines running again on those late afternoons of her next Red Letter Days. There was something about the prospect of changing our jobs and lives—the sense that we could still do something daring, scary, and unconventional—that enlivened us. Our hearts were back in it, as was all our flesh, but as we'd find out a few weeks later when Fran got her period, our renewed determination, without some other factors falling into place, wouldn't get a baby under way.

So Thanksgiving at Fran's parents' was awkward and melancholy, as her mother, who generally evinced an Episcopalian reserve, let slip that someday she'd "just love to have grandchildren around this table," and then asked Fran, "So you're sure about this move? Giving up teaching?

Just like that? And you're so good at it! Your students *love* you!" This, of course, sent Fran into orbit, but it was her mother who first put down her napkin and left the room, as Fran's father, ever the businessman, wondered any number of times about a situation where Fran and I couldn't build equity and have "a place of your own."

At Christmas dinner, my own father said little, as if our plans were too much for him to think about, while my mother had her way of calmly letting us know *exactly* what she was thinking, and, as usual, she was thinking very practically. "Sounds like a wonderful place to be," she said, smiling and serving the cloved ham. "In the summertime," she added. Then, in case we hadn't yet absorbed her meaning: "I wonder where the nearest hospital is up there? Are the schools any good? How cold does it get? And where do you do your shopping?"

A couple days later, our friends and fellow teachers threw a goodbye party, which was more like an *I-bet-you'll-be-back-in-no-time* party, *once you've gotten this out of your systems!* "See you soon," they all said.

Even Fran had her moments of disbelief, if not outright doubt. One morning during our final week of school, we were stuck in traffic on Route 46, as always a few minutes late. In the passenger seat, she was searching in a folder for her lesson plans, when she looked up, startled, and said, "Were we actually up there? Are we really going to do this?"

We did. On the last day of that year, we packed all our earthly belongings, including a folding crib, a flea market special we'd bought the previous spring. Then hill by hill we crawled north again. And just to make matters a little more interesting, there was a dusting of fresh snow on the Thruway at Albany and an inch in Amsterdam. By the time we hit Wells, another inch had accumulated, and it was also getting much colder. At Orma's, icicles hung from the sign and gutters, plastic sheeting covered the windows, and on the dirt road . . . well, it wasn't dirt. Unplowed, the snow blanketed the stones and ruts, and we slithered around the turns. Disconcertingly, we didn't lurch over the bump in the driveway. The snow had leveled that, too. Nor did we immediately recognize the lake. Like everything, it had changed, was indeterminate. Except for the small, vague island, it was a flat, frozen expanse of pale grayness that blended perfectly with the dimming land and sky.

At the door, Abby embraced us warmly and took us through the kitchen and up the narrow back stairway that leads to the innkeepers' quarters, a two bedroom second-floor apartment at the rear of the inn that she called "the annex." By the look of its plain moldings and worn, wall-to-wall carpeting, it was probably added on in the Sixties. Its windows didn't look over the lake, but into the woods, where things seemed more dense and primitive. It had no kitchen—the innkeepers always used the big kitchen below—and the telephone was connected to the main phone in the office. So even up there, you never felt completely private or separated from the inn, though you did feel a little out of the way.

Back down in the kitchen, we ate a late dinner together with Abby. "Happy New Year!" we said, as we listened to the wind lashing the windows, and, on a blurry TV tuned to our single available station, in Utica, we watched the glittering ball drop in Times Square. It seemed a world away.

During the next month, Abby tried to teach us how to be innkeepers. She is one of those good-hearted, independent souls that you often find up here who haven't caught on in a particular vocation, nor tie themselves to someone else for long, and so move from place to place and job to job, a kind of modern nomad, acquiring disparate skills and not seeming to mind the variety. From what I've gathered over the years, she'd grown up in Gloversville in a huge family that didn't or couldn't pay much attention to her or even notice when she was gone. During middle and high school, she worked summers at the inn as a "chore girl." Since then, she'd had jobs in a paint store, a nursery, and office supply shops in Rochester and Syracuse, interspersed with sporadic returns to work here for a week or a couple of months, as if this was always a reliable stop on her wanderings, a place where she was valued. Most recently, she'd been a "digger" at a tree farm, a job that she was now "taking a permanent holiday from," as she said, to decide where to go next, while she helped out at the inn.

Day by day, she walked us through the off-season schedule that she'd been taught by the previous innkeepers. This was how things were *supposed* to happen. On Mondays, you do housekeeping, top to bottom, including stripping the beds—it's laundry pick up day. On Tuesdays, bookkeeping. On Wednesdays, you order meat and fresh produce. On

Thursdays, try to do something fun—relax, gather your strength and wits, call it your "day off." Then on Fridays, if guests have made weekend reservations, get ready, start cooking for real—they'll arrive for dinner. On those Saturdays and Sundays, you're usually going full tilt. You're in the kitchen, you're at the front desk, you're on the phone, you're cleaning up one mess or another. You're tired, frazzled, but you're courteous, cheerful, always smiling. "May I help you?"

Abby made a point of introducing us to what she called "The Regulars," guests we saw on a few weekends that January and would see for longer stays in the summer. She showed us the kitchen set up, her rotation of meals to avoid weekly repetition, her calendar for taking reservations, and her neat account books. All these Fran would manage, while I would try to be "Mr. Repairman" and "Mr. Outside," which at that time of year meant chopping wood and snow removal. Every couple of days, we got a six-inch downfall. As my muscles ached and my back stiffened up like a board, I shoveled the stairs, the porch roof, and a long, deepening trench through the snow between the parking lot and the inn. At great risk of life and limb, Abby showed me how to use the axe and operate the tractor, the latter a skill she'd picked up at that job she'd had at a nursery. Before I eventually got the hang of it, and as Abby, at a respectful distance, watched me plow the parking lot, I flattened any number of shrubs and then impaled the entire tractor, chained rear wheels spinning in the air, on a snow bank of my own making.

That very evening, with the tractor still fixed on the bank, and as Fran was turning baked chicken into smoking charcoal, Mr. Blake called to ask Abby how things were going. "Very well," she told him, giving us a wink.

By mid-month, five feet of snow had piled up. Drifts lapped at the porch railings. Except for the lump that was the boathouse, the lake, the beach, the field, and the knoll were a thick carpet of white. You couldn't walk anywhere outside of a shoveled path without "post-holing." That's when your legs, like posts, sink deep into the snow, and also like posts, they can't move. So one Thursday, Abby taught us how to cross-country ski, to get around *on top* of the snow. "Imagine you're skating," she said, "but keep your feet straight. Push on one foot, glide on the other. Like this."

She skied effortlessly for three or four graceful strides, as if whisked along by a wind I couldn't feel. "Just follow my tracks," she said. And slowly, shakily, with a lot of pushing and little gliding, we managed to follow her route—a full fifty yards!—across the knoll and back.

In the workshop in the basement, Abby showed us all the tools, and every day for the last two weeks of January, she actually gave us *homework*, assigned reading from manuals on plumbing, painting, heating, weatherproofing. Then she made us practice. She broke a windowpane so we could replace it, using a putty knife and glazing compound. We snaked out filthy drains. We countersunk nails and hammered our fingers. We shimmed table legs. With a pencil point and duct tape, we "fixed" a leaky pipe. On another day, Abby and I took off all the doors that stuck in their jambs, and we planed them until I had blisters on my palms, and the doors freely opened and closed—for a week or so.

In an old place like this, nothing is plumb, flush, level, or square. Nothing fits precisely. Nothing is set. Especially in winter, everything is heaving, sagging, twisting, or tilting. So you mend and adjust. You plug and patch. You shim and plane. You take what's given and use what's on hand. You cobble together. You improvise. You can't be daunted by imperfection. You can't make straight all that's warped. You can't make everything new again, or right again, or what carpenters call "true." You can't get back what's gone.

But with a little ingenuity, persistence, and care, you can hold some things together for a while. That's what we learned from Abby.

Then one Monday morning—it seemed so soon!—her scuffed suitcases stood in the hallway next to the door, just like those of any of the guests who'd come and gone during that month. And like those guests, she looked different when she said goodbye. Something in her eyes was miles ahead of her. She had another life to get to. She'd landed a job in Schenectady as a veterinarian's assistant, and she'd be staying with friends while she looked for an apartment there. Instead of her usual gray sweatshirt and lumberjack coat, she wore a mid-length corduroy jacket I hadn't seen before. Her hair, too, had somehow changed, and her boots were suede, came up to her knees, and the heels made her taller.

"I'm hoping to be back next summer for a week of vacation," she said, then quickly added, "but you can call me anytime."

"Let's stay in touch," Fran said. "Thanks for everything." And by the way she held her eyes very still, looking slightly away from Abby, I could tell she was holding back tears.

We all hugged, and each of us took a suitcase outside and down the shoveled path. Abby scraped off her windshield as we loaded in the suitcases. She got behind the wheel of her old, battered Toyota and looked back at the inn. I thought she was going to say, "Take good care of it." But as if she knew more about us than we thought she did, she said, "Take care of yourselves. Good luck."

We waved as she went out the driveway, leaving only our van in the lot. It was one of those bright winter mornings after a snow squall, when everything is still and quiet. Around every tree trunk was a hollow space where the wind had scooped out the snow, and the drifts seemed to smooth every sharpness. Fran and I walked back up the path and up the porch stairs. Now we were on our own. On the mat, while Fran kicked snow from her boots, I hesitated. All the snow, the lake, the forest, the mountain, the inn, even this door I'd passed through hundreds of times already—it all seemed unfamiliar. We were high school teachers, aging New Jersey kids who hadn't grown up. *What the hell are we doing here?*

"You all right?" Fran asked.

I didn't move. It was as though, having come this far, I couldn't take the last step. "Innkeepers? Are we crazy? How are we going to do this, Fran?"

She looked at me in a funny way. She was wearing her puffy green down jacket that made her shoulders look thicker than they were. "Hold out your arms," she said.

"What?"

"Go on, hold them out. Like this."

I held my arms straight out in front of me, and taking my hands, she turned my palms upward. Then she turned her back to me and took a step away. All at once, she fell straight backwards, like a tree toppling, so that, surprised and without even thinking, I had to bend and brace myself to catch her.

"That's how," she said in that definitive, *I'm-glad-we've-settled-that* tone of hers. She had that sort of faith in us. "We'll do whatever we have to."

Now, with her already in my arms, I lifted her up—my wife, all 30 years, 5 feet, 4 inches, and 104 pounds of her—and carried her through the door.

5

Though Fran and I had no basis for comparison then, it turned out to be a pretty easy winter that year, weather-wise, at least. Of course, there was more snow than we'd ever seen, drifts of ten feet on the west side of the porch that climbed halfway up the railings. But the snow came at fairly reasonable intervals, allowing me time to dig out from one storm just before the next arrived.

Even our rookie innkeeper mistakes were more or less manageable, and when they threatened to be otherwise, Fran had a way of looking at guests that made their protestations melt away. Of the two of us, she was by far the better People Person. For our very first visitors, the Blue-line Quilters who came in early February, she cooked up a special "Italian Night" dinner, featuring squid, which she'd bought at a fish market down in Albany. When she got it frying, it stank to high heaven, but having no Plan B, we served it anyway. No one ate it. Everyone nudged the putrid, rubbery stuff to the edges of their plates, and yet when Fran came in smiling, no one complained. The only criticism was a note in our suggestion box: "Everything is wonderful, though you might be a little less ambitious with your entrees."

Other goof-ups also seemed more amusing than mortifying at the time. On another weekend when I was helping Fran serve a pancake breakfast, I somehow filled the syrup pitcher with coffee, so that our guests had the pleasure of mixing on their plates what they might rather have mixed in their stomachs. And then there was that afternoon when I lost my footing on the porch roof while shoveling off another load of snow. Like a kid on a slide, I shot downhill into open air, then flew feet first into one of those monster snow drifts, post-holing myself to the armpits. Naturally, this happened on a weekday when there were no guests, no staff, and soon after Fran had gone to Orma's to pick up some odds and ends and have a nice long chat with whoever was there. For more than a half hour, I was stuck in that drift, increasingly concerned about my bathroom options, and when Fran finally returned—before she cried, "Man overboard!" and threw me a rope—her first words of wifely sympathy were, "Goodness, Mark, you seem to have lost something in stature!"

That winter we also met most of the "Year-Rounders," the people, like Orma, who really lived, not just visited, in the hamlets or on the roads around the lake: Zeke and Ada Perkins, Luke Trim, Dave Debar, Wes Magoon, our postmistress Flora Haskell, and our sheriff Jim Owen. Most of their families had been in the area for generations. Their forebearers hunted, trapped, logged, and worked in the sawmills and small tanning factories in the valleys. Now, many women stood behind counters in souvenir shops and pine-paneled restaurants during the summers, or checked out groceries and sold Lotto tickets at the market in Speculator. The men plowed roads for the county all winter, and during the other seasons, they hauled lumber for Stephenson's, or sanded and varnished at LeBlec's Boat Repair, or they worked at anything, jacks of all trades, depending on what needed doing. On the right side of Orley Tuttle's rusted-out truck it said, "Level Best Carpentry," and on the left, "Royal Flush Plumbing," both with the same phone number.

How did we fit in? Well, we were certainly the odd birds in the area. We didn't hunt or ice fish. We didn't—and I still don't—have a snowmobile. We were Out-of-Staters, perhaps even worse than Down-Staters, and here we were, brand new, with full-year jobs, an unusual thing in these parts. So I'd be lying if I said we didn't feel some unspoken suspicion and resentment directed our way. Especially in the early days, a number of people regarded us from a distance. A few didn't seem too friendly. But winters here have a way of eroding differences. If you've ever seen people picking their way through a driving snowstorm, you'll know what I mean. Bundled up in a face mask, down parka, snow pants, boots, and mittens the size of boxing gloves, all your peculiarity goes out the window. Everyone looks about the same. Everyone's concerns are about the same. Everyone just wants to get home and warm. Everyone leans into the wind.

"How you doing?" was the usual greeting we'd get at the bi-weekly Friday night potluck dinners at Orma's that we'd go to when we didn't have guests. And most folks there, sitting around the rickety card tables, seemed genuinely interested, as well as vaguely amused by us. In time, we made some friends, especially Bruce and Lena Wagoner, who were about our age, both broad-faced and thick-limbed, from old Adirondack logging families, though they'd managed to get away to college at SUNY Binghamton, where they'd met. From June through September, Bruce was the ranger at the public campground a few miles down the lakeshore, and he was the guy who had noticed our tractor stranded on the snow bank and towed it out with his Ford Bronco. Afterward, we invited him in for coffee. He wore boots, of course, and insulated overalls with many pockets, along with a red plaid cap with earflaps that made him look like a big, rosy-cheeked schoolboy. He said he and Lena had five kids between two and eleven. She was the county's part-time visiting librarian during the school year, and as it happened, Fran and I ran into her at the market a few days later. She was hauling one kid in a backpack, who was pulling her hair, while another, in full tantrum, kicked and screamed in the child's seat of her grocery cart. Amid this mayhem, Lena looked at us with her soft eyes and said, almost calmly, "You're Fran and Mark. From the Tumble Inn, right? You should come over some night, if you don't mind the chaos. How about tomorrow?"

And so began our regular evenings with the Wagoners at their small log home near Sand Point, about a mile away. There, as their kids ran around and practically pulled down the curtains, we played cards, drank Saranac ale, and swapped stories. They were indeed a chaotic family, yet a family nonetheless, and we were part of it when we were with them. Their second-to-youngest, Joey, would climb on our laps, spill milk on our jeans, or tie our laces to the table legs. Meanwhile, the oldest ones, Tom, Riley, and the middle one, Jill, would tease and yell and wrestle with each other. You'd think this would have driven us crazy, this glut of children we didn't have, and yes, there was pain, pain that Lena and Bruce could plainly see in our faces. Yet they weren't about to keep us at a distance, nor hide their children from us. Once, when their kids were so wild that Bruce sent them all outside to play in the snow for fifteen minutes, it got weirdly quiet indoors. You could hear logs shifting in the stove and the kettle steaming on top of it. The room, though we were in it, felt suddenly desolate, and I recall Lena looking at Fran and me with such fierce sympathy and understanding, as if she might *will* a child into Fran's womb.

I guess that's what we most appreciated about the Wagoners: that capacity they had for sympathy. We needed it. As you might have predicted, our change of residence, like our renewed determination, didn't automatically change our luck in getting a baby going.

"Maybe next month," Fran had said when her period came again near the end of January.

"We'll keep at it," I replied. Both of us were trying to sound optimistic, though there was also frustration and fear in our voices. Back in August, our doctors in New Jersey, after testing an unnerving array of bodily fluids, had found no obvious reason why we couldn't conceive.

"So why the hell isn't anything happening?" Fran asked me any number of times, knowing I had no answer. "Meanwhile, the clock is ticking!"

She could, of course, with a doctors' okay, have begun a regime of fertility drugs, involving hypodermic needles, routine trips to a hospital in Albany, and scads of money that we'd have to borrow from our parents. But at that point, we weren't so desperate, or so we told ourselves.

In fact, in the last days of February we had good reason for hope. We were making breakfast for ourselves one slow Monday, when Fran, breaking eggs into a bowl, said casually, "It's late."

I thought she was referring to the weekly laundry pick up, the panel truck that comes about eleven o'clock, when we'd need to have all the used sheets and pillowcases ready to go. So I said, "No, it's early yet. It's only eight-thirty. There's no rush."

She looked at me like I was from outer space. "I mean *my period*. It's two days late, and it usually comes on time. Perhaps, if you remember some things from your Health class, you might see some possible meaning in this."

I tried not to look thrown off balance. "Well, if you think you might be pregnant, why don't you check it out with your indicator thing?" Upstairs in our medicine cabinet, Fran had a home pregnancy test kit with a fancy little stick which, when dipped in urine, magically produced a plus or a minus sign.

"That won't be accurate for a few days," she said. "Thursday at the earliest. Then, to confirm a positive, we'll have to see the doctor at the clinic." The health clinic was over in Speculator.

So for the rest of that Monday and the following Tuesday and Wednesday, we went about our chores in a kind of anxious suspension, trying not to get our hopes up, trying not to talk about it, but talking about it and getting our hopes up nonetheless.

"I've had dreams," Fran said as we lay in bed on that Wednesday night. Still, her period hadn't come, and neither of us could fall right to sleep. "Sometimes I hear light breathing from the other bedroom, or someone shaking something, like seeds in a dried gourd, or a rattle. It sounds almost like rain on the window, but when I wake up of course it's not raining. It's not even snowing or hailing."

As for me, I didn't dream of anything like this. I don't think I dreamed at all. But during those days, I'd worked with a strange, wild energy, chopping wood and stacking so much of it on the porch that you could hardly get in and out of the door. "Who do you think you are?" Fran asked, "Paul Bunyan?"

When I woke up that Thursday morning, however, everything had changed. Fran wasn't in bed beside me. I got up in the dim light and went into our living area and then into the other bedroom, where we'd stashed the folded-up crib and some boxes we hadn't yet unpacked. Fran wasn't in there either. Then, from the bathroom on the other side of the hall, came the sound of soft weeping.

The door was closed and I went to it. I said, "Fran?" but she didn't reply. I said her name again, then knocked lightly. Still, she didn't say anything. "You okay?" But there was just that soft weeping and snagging breath, like the sound a small animal might make.

"Did you do the test?" I asked, afraid she'd gotten a negative result.

After some time, she finally said in a trembling voice, "No. I didn't have to."

"What do you mean? Your period came?"

"Yes. I think so. Well, no, I'm not sure. It's all different." Then she was weeping again.

For a time, I tried to understand what she was saying, and later that morning, Dr. Floyd, probably seeing the look in Fran's face, said to both of us in his office at the clinic, "I won't try to fool you. You probably had what's called a 'chemical pregnancy' and a very early miscarriage. It's not uncommon, though most women don't notice it and doctors seldom call attention to it. It's one of those things that sometimes is best kept secret. It requires no medical treatment. A fertilized egg fails to implant on the uterine wall, and so it's washed away in what usually seems like a normal menstrual period that's perhaps a little heavy and late."

At the word "fails," Fran flinched and her jaw tightened. Then, holding herself very straight and still, and looking the doctor in the eye, she said, "So I was pregnant for a very short time?"

"I can't be absolutely sure," he replied, "but that, by far, is the most likely explanation. I wish I had better news."

In silence, I drove slowly and carefully back to the inn, while Fran sat with her head tilted to the side and her eyes staring blankly through the windshield.

So we'd conceived, I kept thinking. *A swirl of cells. And before we knew it: gone.*

"No one's giving up," Fran said as we got out of the van. "But Mark, I don't know how long I can stand this."

More than ever then, we were living double lives, and only at certain moments with the Wagoners did those lives intersect. On the one hand, there was our private life as husband and wife yearning to be parents, while on the other were our more public lives as members of a small Adirondack community, as innkeepers, as friends, and as children of our own parents.

At the beginning of March, we had two free weekends, and though we weren't really in the mood for company, we went ahead and gave our parents the green light to visit. Not so subtly, they'd been suggesting this since we'd left New Jersey, concerned as they were about what we'd gotten ourselves into. Fran's parents came the first weekend, her mother helping in the kitchen, though you could tell by her pursed lips and a certain determined way that she cut carrots that she was keeping her feelings to herself. Fran's father, however, immediately fell in love with the place. He admired all the tools hanging on pegboard over the workbench in the basement. He studied the heating and water systems. "Fascinating!" he said. On the porch, he couldn't keep his eyes off the view. In a closet, he found an old pair of snowshoes and, in his heavy, hooded jacket, went tramping around on the knoll.

As for my own father, we barely heard a peep from him on the following weekend after he'd lowered himself into the rocking chair beside the fire, with his newspaper on his lap. He wasn't being rude. He was just being his usual mild, phlegmatic self, the sort of guy you don't notice though he's sitting right beside you. "Rudeness," as my mother always explained, "presumes an awareness of your surroundings and a degree of conscious activity, not exactly his strongest suits!"

Of course, conscious activity *was* her strong suit. After breakfast, she announced that she was going out shopping. It hardly mattered that she was in the middle of the Adirondack wilderness. With her list in her navy blue purse, she was out the door and into her Buick, fishtailing up the driveway. By early evening, she was back with armloads of boxes, bags, and packages, having had her way at the mall in Albany. She'd bought quarts of Windex and furniture polish, a half dozen new lampshades, cubic feet of potpourri, two fruit baskets, and enough dried flower arrangements to start a boutique. She was making herself comfortable here.

On the other hand, Howie Sanders, our histrionic friend and teaching colleague from back at Garfield High, was nothing but miserable when he came during the next week, his spring vacation, which was still dead winter in these parts. He hated the snow. All the open space made him nervous. "It's a barren wilderness!" he declared with his usual tact and subtlety, and he spent much of his visit curled and shivering beneath layers of quilts, coughing and snuffling. To make matters worse, his life back home was "in shambles." "I'm burning out," he said one evening, all swaddled up on the bed in his room. "I'm as bad as the students. I barely teach my classes anymore."

"Then leave!" Fran said with her own brand of tact and subtlety. Maybe, inadvertently, that word "barren" had struck a nerve.

"And do what?"

"Anything you want."

"Well, I can't run off and be an innkeeper, for example. A place like this would kill me." He coughed and snuffled. "It might already be killing me!"

Fran had no patience for this. Those weeks she was not the most hospitable innkeeper. "Buck up, Howie. Get a grip. You've got a cold, for crying out loud!"

What I most want to remember about that winter, however—and what I most want to keep remembering—is that even as we were hurting and yearning, Fran and I managed to put one foot in front of the other, and, all things considered, we hung together pretty well. Everything seemed new, often overwhelming and frightening, but we were alive to it all. As innkeepers, we adapted, or we tried to. To hosannas, we served spaghetti and meatballs for "Italian Night" dinners. To prevent more breakfast adventures on my part, we labeled one pitcher "Syrup" and another "Coffee." With a rope through an open window, I tethered myself to a bedpost whenever I shoveled the porch roof. With an infinitude of patience, Bruce Wagoner picked up where Abby had left off and gave me pointers as, ham-handed, I learned to use the Skilsaw, the power drill, and the electric sander. It took me all day and a number of tries, but I eventually replaced a broken step on the basement stairs and the leg of a coffee table. And against stiff odds, Fran and I actually got better at cross-country skiing, though I wouldn't have called us remotely proficient. Any slope, uphill or down, was fraught with danger, and turning usually meant calamity. Still, we kept trying, and once, by a round-about route, we made our way down to the lake and onto the wide, frozen surface. We went out five or six hundred yards, halfway to the island, where the wind had swept whorls in the snow. Far ahead in the whiteness, we saw the ice shanties, shaped like outhouses, that fishermen had dragged to the middle of the lake. Through the third week of March, the ice remained thick enough to support them, though to us it still felt eerie to be out there, as if we were testing our trust. All that water below. All that distance from shore. Now and then, we came across long, zigzagging cracks through the packed snow, and sometimes we heard the ice make a deep, vibrating, *thwonk*-ing sound, like when you wobble a piece of sheet metal.

Eventually, we made a wide loop that brought the inn again into view. Against the gray-white mountains and sunk into the drifts, it looked so small and squat, a disappearing thing, an unpromising place for our dreams. It seemed more to huddle than stand up on that knoll, all its edges and angles worn away. Yet it had a certain stubbornness up there, a way of persisting by burrowing and waiting, biding its time and not giving in.

As we stood, looking, our chests were heaving, Fran's cheeks pink, her breath white on her scarf, and sprouts of sweaty red hair frosted along the edge of her wool cap. She was exhausted, and she, especially, was dispirited by our inability to conceive. But her eyes still had that eagerness in them, that spark when you least expected it. "Race you back," she said after a moment. And not waiting for my reply: "Ready. Set. Go!"

Then we scrambled forward, falling and getting up, following our tracks across the ice, over the field, around the knoll, and back toward the closest thing to what we'd call a home, though of course it wasn't really ours.

6

It begins imperceptibly, usually by mid-March, when the very last of the winter guests have gone. There's a thinning and softening of the ice on the lake. It must happen more on the bottom of the ice than on the top which, at least to my eye, doesn't seem to change at all. But then one day, you glance out one of the living room windows, and something feels different. Something's missing. You pick up the binoculars, scan the surface, and you realize that the little fishing shanties are all gone, dragged away, and the only thing still out there is a single forty-gallon beer keg, filled with sand or concrete.

About the same time, a coffee can appears beside the cash register at Orma's, with a sign taped to the front:

ALL BETS ($5 PER PERSON)
DUE APRIL 1 (NO FOOLING!)

By that date, about a hundred dollars' worth of experience, intuition, calculation, and hope will have piled up in the can, every cent of it to go to the lucky winner who comes closest to guessing the date when the keg will fall through the ice, our clearest sign that spring might actually come. On a sheet of paper beside the can, everyone records their guesses for public scrutiny and debate. That year Fran guessed April 8, a rookie mistake, a record for giddy optimism, and I chose April 15 for no other reason than that's when certain other important things are due. Most others chose times during the week of April 23, when historically your chances are best. But Alvah Flanders, who lives way up Haskell's Road and calls himself an "individualist socialist," hit the jackpot by choosing May 1, May Day, which was in fact the day when the keg fell through, making Alvah a rich socialist, until he spent it all buying rounds that night at the Oxbow, where the keg had come from in the first place.

Now things on the lake started happening faster and all in plain view. The ice turned spongy and gray. We didn't dare ski or stand on it. Soon it crept away from the shore, leaving a band of open water. Next, holes and cracks appeared on the surface, with water on top and pushing through from underneath, making dark pools and crisscrossed channels. The remaining ice changed from gray to black and looked pocked or honeycombed. Beginning near the shore, it broke into smaller drifting chunks that melted or sank. Then—incredibly!—by that same afternoon, the lake was altogether clear, so bright and blue that it hurt your eyes, and it was ribbed and moving. With waves!

But the blue water, like a tease, didn't last. Weeks of bleak, sodden weather immediately followed, our "mud season," when spring seems indefinitely postponed. Wet snow alternates with icy rain. The snowpack melts, freezes, and remelts. The driveway washes out. The bridge on the dirt (that is, mud) road floods, then ices over.

During this time, when, thank God, we're always closed for business, the inn itself becomes a swamped vessel. On the roof, water backs up behind ice dams, leaks around flashing, and seeps down walls upstairs. In the basement, jets of groundwater spurt through the foundation, making a kind of bilge. Meanwhile, the brook in the woods becomes a raging torrent, having burst out of the ice that had encased it for months. It hurls huge ice slabs over its banks, along with boulders and uprooted trees. As for the lake, its level rises ominously, covering the beach and almost surrounding the boathouse. On stormy days, waves break *over* the dock, carrying with them a thick mat of stinking *mundungus*, the Indian name for the decomposing leaves and other filth that our sylvan lake disgorges on the beach each spring.

So while the rest of the world bathes in Easter sunshine, we are besieged by water and muck. The skies are slate-colored. So is the lake. There's no hope, no resurrection. Everyone's cooped-up, climbing the walls, by turns lethargic then borderline murderous, and I'm sad to say that Fran and I were no exceptions. Our baby-making activities over the last couple of months were less pleasurable, more mechanical, more freighted again with our imperative to be fruitful and multiply, and when Fran's period arrived around the third week of May, we were at each other like rival tomcats. As "the *supposed* man of the house," "the *so-called* Mr. Outside and Mr. Repairman," I wasn't "pulling my weight" anymore, she said. I'd become "Mr. Wait-Until-Summer" or "Mr. Sit-by-the-Fire, like your father!" The grounds, she went on, were "a mess." Branches down. The driveway impassible.

So what was I supposed to do? Go outside with an umbrella and say, "Please rain, stop, so I can clean up?" Or maybe I should put on my swimming trunks—no, a wetsuit!—and try to round up the mundungus? "If you feel so strongly about it," I said one gray afternoon as we sat in the downstairs living room, "why don't *you* go out there? You're not exactly Mrs. Dynamo yourself these days! Reading catalogues in bed for half the morning! And whose brilliant idea was it to come up here in the first place? So we could have jobs we know nothing about? So we could experience this lovely spring in the Adirondacks? What in God's name were you thinking—that snow, mud, and mildewed walls would fix whatever's wrong and help us make a baby? This isn't *my* fault, you know!"

You'd think I'd slapped her in the face, which I guess, metaphorically speaking, I had. Chin on knees and hands squeezed between her thighs, she shriveled down into the sofa. Her silence said everything. Livid with self-reproach, I stomped out through the kitchen and up the back stairs.

We went on like this for another week or so, a regular Adirondack mud season couple. Then, eventually, the rain slackened, the brook confined itself to its banks, the lake receded inch by inch, and I managed to get myself out on the beach where I raked the mundungus into piles, shoveled it into the cart behind the tractor, and hauled it to the compost heap in the woods. Meanwhile, Fran started washing the musty curtains and quilts in the guest rooms, and one evening while I was trying to fix a leaky faucet upstairs and she was cleaning up in the kitchen, we heard something that made us go out on the porch together. From somewhere on the lake, came the calls of loons, that wild laughter and those lonesome, mournful wails bouncing off the hills and mountains, echoing and entwining.

The loons, it seemed, had returned from wherever they'd spent the winter. We spotted a pair of them swimming low on the water, gliding softly and mysteriously, their heads curved like the handles of canes, their bills moving like scissors. And I think it was while we listened to and watched the loons—watched them diving, disappearing, then whole minutes later reappearing, on the water—that most of the spite we had left drained out of us, and we were more or less ourselves again.

Soon other birds—sparrows, wrens, red-winged blackbirds—woke us in the mornings. One evening, we made it over to the Wagoners' to play cards, and on Memorial Day weekend, we heard the first motorboats sputtering to life, then buzzing like mosquitoes. A few guests had made reservations: bird-watchers with fancy cameras and tripods, and fishermen anxious to get a start on the new season, loaded with tackle boxes, rods, nets, and bulging camouflage vests. At night, specks of light glimmered on the shore: summer residents checking up on their cottages to see what the winter had wrought.

That weekend we also beheld a miracle, three solid days of sun, and everything exploded with life, as if the chance might never come again. Trees leafed out. Ferns unfurled. The knoll got shaggy. A yellow-green wave of new foliage raced up the mountain, and in the evenings, as the light was dimming, we heard peepers off in a bog in the woods, that faint, high-pitched, almost electrical twanging, like sounds from another world.

Then on the following Tuesday, after the guests had gone, Fran and I hiked up the brook. It wasn't a planned outing. In fact, just a few words, a look in Fran's eye, and that way, with her finger, she slowly traced a vein on the back of my wrist—that's what made it all happen. We'd finished our lunch at the kitchen table, when she reached out and touched me like that. Then looking straight at me, she said, "Mark, I wonder what's up the brook."

After that, "up the brook" would become a kind of code for us. "You feel like going up the brook?" she'd ask in that same shy yet insistent way. How could I ever say no? Even now, all these years later, "up the brook," just that phrase, melts something inside me.

On that afternoon, the temperature must have broken into the seventies—uncharted territory!—and we were wearing exotic clothes: light sweatshirts and wrinkled shorts that we'd exhumed from the backs of bureau drawers. With the air wafting against our reborn legs, we walked out the driveway and across the road to where the trail begins and winds toward the woods through a field of blueberry bushes. In the woods, the air was cooler, the sun sifted into dancing dots, and the ground was springy with pine needles and leaf mold. We climbed up a gentle hillside of hemlocks and swamp maples that led to higher stands of spruce and pine. Ahead, we could hear the brook getting louder, a tumbling sound. We picked up our pace. Ferns, still unfurling, brushed our shins. The trillium and wild azalea were blooming. Black mushrooms had poked up their heads. Everything smelled rich and alive, and then we came to the water.

The brook, in this stretch, is a classic Adirondack mountain stream: clean, clear, and very purposeful, especially in the spring. It doesn't bother with whirlpools and eddies. It certainly doesn't meander. It has things to do, appointments to keep. It rushes around and over rocks and logs, if it can't push them out of its way.

On its east side, we followed the narrow path under limbs, over gnarled roots, and, grasping onto saplings and bushes, we edged step by step along the bank as it got steeper. Soon the only way up was in the middle of the brook, scrambling from boulder to boulder.

We took off our sweatshirts and tied them around our waists. The backs of our T-shirts were soaked. Our skin, cocooned for months in wool and flannel, was the creamy color of the underside of fungi that grow on fallen trees. Without stopping, Fran rolled her short sleeves up to her armpits. We were breathing hard now. We seemed to be racing. As we climbed, the brook got narrower, louder, and faster, rolling in crested standing waves, pouring through gaps between mounded boulders, or charging headlong over ledges, then roiling into bubbles and foam.

Further on, though, it leveled off, quieted, seeming to pause before its wild descent, and fanned across a wide, domed, mossy rock in an open swath of sunshine.

We stopped. Except for a huge, uprooted birch lodged between the banks a few feet above the water, there were only us, the rock, and the sky. We stood face to face, beneath a big open space in the trees, exposed, where nothing could be hidden.

Fran had always described herself as a feminist, "a feminist of the heterosexual persuasion," and as you must have already gathered, she had no aversion to taking the wheel when she knew where she wanted to go. So it won't surprise you that, with an idea firmly in mind, she reached up with both hands, pulled my head toward her, and kissed me in a way that, to put it mildly, achieved its optimum effect.

Instantly, we were pulling at each other's sweaty, clinging shirts, shorts, and underwear, and soon, except for our soggy socks and boots, we stood there in all our glory: boney hips, pointy elbows, and patches of kinky hair.

We did those things that you do with your hands. Groping. Fumbling. Getting it somewhat right. Then, as if to luxuriate, to both hold and hasten the moment, we lay down on the soft, water-swept moss. It was a beautiful, romantic, pastoral impulse, a thing for shepherds and shepherdesses, or even for lumberjacks and gritty girlfriends, but not quite a thing for us. The frigid water undid our handiwork. The moss felt like slime. So we were up again, at work again, in a slightly different rustic venue. With her back against the curved trunk of the uprooted birch, Fran sort of reclined, sort of hiked herself up with one leg and one elbow, while I, facing her, sort of draped myself over her, with my arms clamped around her bottom and the toes of my boots wedged against the rock.

In this novel position, unreported in "How To" manuals, we slipped, slithered, and lost our balance, but eventually, like a cold engine that finally gets cranking, we gained headway again, warming up, moving together, our skin getting clammy in the sun.

Then in our ears and from all around us, came a perplexing, low humming sound. But it wasn't a hummingbird. It wasn't bees. It couldn't have been motorboats or helicopters. It wasn't even mosquitoes, or anything we'd ever known.

If you've lived through a spring in the Adirondacks, or even if you've only exchanged pleasantries with someone here during that season, then you'll know about blackflies. They lay their eggs by the millions in swift-flowing water. Their wormy, gooey, comma-shaped larvae grow on submerged rocks. As one, they hatch and emerge as full adults: small, humpbacked, strong-jawed, stocky as linemen, hungry, and on the wing. They rove in packs, seeking flesh, preferring areas of moisture and warmth where blood pulses near the surface. Clothing and fur offer little protection. Hair offers none. With barbed legs, they affix themselves like Velcro, and unlike a mosquito's surgical drilling, they chew and excavate, strip mining, and, craving more, they hold on for dear life.

At the moment they landed, Fran and I, too, had affixed ourselves. Our hands were occupied. Our skins flushed. To the flies, my ass must have looked like a gleaming, white peach, and they must have thought they were born into paradise.

I wish I could say that we surrendered to them, but "surrender" presumes more thought and free will than were available at the moment. Our will was otherwise engaged. If I thought at all, if I could have willed anything into being, it would have been to have grown a tail, a long, swishing horse's tail, with which I could have casually brushed off the flies.

As it was, we were helpless. I had no tail. The flies had their way. And you'd think that Fran and I would have instantly untangled ourselves, then, madly itching and swatting, trying to keep our private parts from public consumption, we'd have run for the nearest depth of water, and plunged our sorry selves in.

But that's not how it happened. As the flies bit into us, as the pain multiplied, Fran and I, with even *more* intensity, dug deeper into one another. It was as if, in our pleasure, we were trying to keep ahead of the pain, less to outrun than to outlast and outlive it, and surely not to ignore it. It was as if we were trying to take it all in, every bite and excavation, and somehow turn it to our advantage. With the flies ravishing us, we poured every last bit of ourselves into saving us, or at least that's how it seemed. Only after the flies were done with us were Fran and I done with each other.

Then as suddenly as they'd come, the flies, en masse, moved away upstream, perhaps to rest their jaws and digest, to have a smoke and put up their feet. It was quiet, except for the brook sliding over the rock. Trembling, Fran and I peeled ourselves from the fallen tree. We stood before one another, husband and wife, still beneath the bright, exacting sun, with our clothes scattered like blown trash. We were covered with small, red, bleeding dots—more dots than Fran had freckles—and each was upheld on a swelling mound of pink flesh.

"At least we had the sense to keep our boots on," Fran said, and we smiled, but mostly on the inside. The flies seemed to have found particular pleasure behind our knees, on our necks, in the crooks of our arms, and in the soft flesh around our mouths. So when we moved, even to smile, we were stiff and slow, like rusted farm equipment. Our eyes were puffing up. My ass was on fire, and this still astounds me: a couple of flies, brave as sperm, must have squeezed, squiggled, and swum their way into the act itself. For that part of me that had labored in the deep and dark, most hidden and protected, was now oddly bumped out on one side, re-swollen as it were, like an inner tube with a weak spot.

"You look lopsided!" Fran just had to point out. "Poor fellow."

"All right," I said, cutting her off. "What tonic you are for my self-esteem."

But looking back, I don't begrudge any of it: not the fun poked my way, not all the itching and scratching, not even the lopsidedness that made urinating a wayward adventure, not even the three days when it took a half hour to get dressed, when I walked bowlegged, when at Orma's we got the strangest looks—*What the hell happened to you?*—and when at nights we marinated in witch hazel and Rhulicream, and still didn't sleep a wink. . . .

No, I don't begrudge it. I'd do it all again.

As I've mentioned, we hadn't ever seen or heard of blackflies at the time, so guessing, we called them gnats.

"If anything—if anyone—comes of this," Fran said as we gingerly put on our clothes, "I guess we'll have to call him Nat."

I saw my chance to get back at my hetero-feminist wife a little. "Or we'll have to call *her* Natalie," I said.

June up here is a busy month. Every year, spring lasts a week or two, and then all at once full-fledged summer is upon us. The finches start gibbering. The mountain turns a deep, forest green. The field blossoms with white daisies. On the lake, mergansers skitter in the weeds, and on weekends motor boats cut across the surface, and a few little white triangles of sail glide around where the ice fishing shanties had stood. All this is good and pleasing to the soul, though day by day, you can feel something else, almost hear it like a faint but growing undertone, like the distant approach of a ragged army. And you can see it too, right there on the office calendar, beginning when schools let out at the end of the month: rank upon rank of full week reservations—the Regulars!—nearly wall-to-wall through Labor Day.

With just three weeks before they'd start arriving that summer, the place was still a mess. All those things that we couldn't or didn't do in the mud season were clamoring for our attention. Jack up the porch roof that sagged like a saddle. Regrade the driveway. Replace rotted boards on the boathouse dock. Clean and caulk the canoes. Unhook the storm windows. Hook in the screens. And did I mention that the mundungus was still washing up on the beach? Or that the porch furniture in the basement was lacy with cobwebs?

We were up at five-thirty. To bed no earlier than eleven. Our Thursday "days off" went by the wayside. Between the two of us—and trying to remember what Abby had taught us—Fran and I raked, mowed, washed linens and grimy windows, waxed floors, hauled trash, planted annuals, pruned limbs, bleached, scoured, drilled, sawed, shimmed, sanded, leveled, braced, nailed . . . and screwed, by which I refer only to the act of fastening with a screwdriver. There was no time to even think of the other activity.

Though, as always, there was time to *screw up*. In our haste, we added mineral spirits to water-based paint, yielding something like cottage cheese. Then, after buying another fresh couple of gallons, we painted ourselves into corners of rooms and had to leave through the nearest window, once stranding ourselves on the porch roof.

And there was the issue of our summer "help." For jobs in our quaint and tasteful hospitality business, we interviewed dour, acned high school boys and countless chatty, high-octane girls who chewed gum and said "you know" at least twice per sentence. Eventually we settled on two saucy, klutzy, absent-minded twin sisters, Bridgette and Brittany Busby—"The Killer Bees," we called them—to wait tables and do the housekeeping when they weren't fixing their frizzy hair. Then, to assist me with the outside work, we hired Zack, a painfully shy sixteen-year-old string bean of a kid, who the Bees teased mercilessly. And Robert (not Rob, Bob, Robby or Bobby—he took himself *very* seriously) was our summer cook, or rather our "chef," as he insisted. He even wore one of those puffy white hats.

So with our first summer staff now assembled and whipped into shape in two frantic days of so-called "training," on a Friday evening in the third week of the month, the first minivans of Regulars came *ker-thunk*ing over the unrepaired bump in the driveway. Screaming, cooped-up kids spewed from doors and charged up the front stairs. Weary parents dragged in heaps of luggage. And right in the middle of this, at about nine o'clock, we got a phone call from Mr. Blake telling us the sad news that Mr. Dunning had died, and that he, Mr. Blake, was the new president and chair of the board. He wished us a good summer season and said he looked forward to the improved service and standards of the inn when he and his family would come for their vacation in August.

Bleary-eyed, Fran and I stayed up a few more hours to welcome the late arrivals. With all this going on, we didn't sleep long or well that night, and naturally it was on that very next morning, or still in the milky blue hours before dawn, that Fran sat up in bed and started heaving, with nausea, gas, headache, the works.

"This could be it!" she said between gasps. She seemed thrilled to be feeling so rotten.

"What?"

"Morning sickness!"

"Well, is your period late?"

"Jesus. What day is it?"

"The twenty-third."

"Yes! It's late enough!"

"Then see what the indicator says."

"Screw that," she said. "We're going straight to the clinic!"

"Look, it's five a.m., and in two hours someone has to serve eggs, muffins, and bacon here. It's not like you're having a baby right now!"

"We'll be back by six. I'm calling Dr. Floyd. Get dressed."

Confronted with the full force of Fran's forward momentum, neither I nor Dr. Floyd had a chance. Twenty minutes later, we met him at the clinic on Route 8, he unshaved, his hair uncombed, me still groggy, and Fran holding a small Hellmann's mayonnaise jar containing an inch of her bright and exquisitely named "early morning urine," as if it was liquid gold.

The doctor mixed some of it with chemicals in a test tube. He shook it and, squinting, held it up to the florescent light. "It's positive," he said in his matter-of-fact way, showing us the brownish-tan solution. It could have been apple cider.

Fran and I were both quiet. After all the zigzags on the ovulation charts, all the careening hopes and disappointments, all the pleasures and *plain hard work*, not to mention the blackflies—after all that, the moment seemed strangely ordinary. Like learning that you have a package waiting at the post office.

"Could you say that again?" Fran asked the doctor. She was smoothing her denim skirt across her legs.

"It's positive. You're pregnant." Then after a moment, he asked, "How do you feel?"

Fran stared at me as if she both believed and didn't believe him, though the believing part was getting stronger. That might have been the only time in her life when words didn't immediately come to her. Nor did they come to me. She just kept staring like that, with tears forming in the corners of her eyes, until, referring I suppose to any number of things, she said, "What I feel right now is . . . full."

While it was what we'd desperately wanted to accomplish, there couldn't have been a worse time for Fran to have gotten "knocked up," as she liked to say, right at the beginning of our first summer here. We called our parents with our news, then decided to hold off telling anyone else, even our friends the Wagoners, until after the first trimester, when we'd have a better sense of how this pregnancy was going. As you might imagine, our parents, especially our mothers, were excited and wanted to visit, but there were no vacant rooms until September. And *we* certainly weren't going anywhere. The inn was jammed. No let up. So many people. So many things to keep track of. Reservations. Brimming trash. Unmown grass. Laundry. Broken china. Spiders in room #5. A toilet overflowing. Someone has hives. Someone's hearing aid is in the salad! Someone needs ice. Pronto!

On the Fourth of July, we had the annual cookout, with hotdogs and hamburgers crammed on the grill, heaps of coleslaw, potato salad, corn on the cob, and a busted underground water pipe that made a geyser beside the swing set. Sometime that July we also had our first big electrical storm. The gray clouds poured over the mountain. Zack, the Bees, and I raced around closing windows. Through horizontal rain, we chased rocking chairs across the porch and lugged them inside. The lights blinked and went out. The toilets flushed once and wouldn't refill, and of course I hadn't yet learned to operate the generator, so, for a stretch of about twelve hours, the bathrooms had a distinct air about them.

Meanwhile, Fran's morning sickness came at the most inconvenient moments: mornings, afternoons, and/or evenings. For example, on the hottest day of the summer, we were madly scooping strawberry ice cream from the big canisters into thirty bowls, so that Bridgette could hustle the desserts into the dining room before they'd melt into pools. That's precisely when Fran started feeling sick. Sometimes, I think, she just wanted to get away from the chaos, something for which I had less sympathy at the moment than I do now when I look back on it. In the midst of things, she dropped her metal scoop, turned, and took herself up to the annex to lie down and read for a while.

We could never have made it through the last weeks of that August had not Abby been among the guests. On her first day, she strode into the kitchen, glanced around, assessed the dire situation, then grabbed an apron off the hook on the back of the door. "All right, let's get to it," she said, and for her entire "vacation," she insisted on helping out. With Robert, she dug into the mountain of dirty dishes. She browbeat the Bees into folding napkins, emptying wastebaskets, and taking out the trash. At the reception desk, she kept track of canoe rentals while answering the phone, cradling it in the crook of her neck as she punched keys on the calculator.

During that summer, we met all the Regulars, as their families came and went in tidal waves: the Halseys, the Fraziers, the Biswangers, the Pendletons, and the ever-burgeoning Murphy clan, to name but a few. Three, sometimes four, generations of a family would gather here, and for a week everyone on the premises would have curly hair and ears that stuck out. Then the next week, you'd only see fair skin and high cheek bones. And the week after that—these would be the Biswangers—everyone wore glasses and had big feet. We'd have loved to get to know them all better, and we *did* try to socialize after breakfast or dinner, but something was always coming up and we'd be running off to put out fires.

By that Labor Day weekend, things were downright feverish and out of control. During one dinner, Brittany took Robert's motto of "stick-to-the-ribs cooking" too literally by losing her balance and spilling a full gravy boat onto the Oxford shirt of none other than Mr. Blake. Not a few times, I lost my temper with the Bees, and I also remember losing it with Fran, when one morning I found a flood on the kitchen floor—she'd forgotten to close the freezer. At night, bottle rockets shrieked up from the knoll. Teenagers snuck off in canoes for the island, colliding and capsizing along the way. By day, we tended to scraped knees, sprained ankles, and at least one case of heat exhaustion. The lake teemed with roaring motorboats and suicide skiers, like drag racers on the water.

So it was startling to wake on the following Tuesday and hear . . . almost nothing! Just the slightest breeze rustling the leaves and the ascending and tumbling songs of the warblers. On the porch the rocking chairs were empty and still. There wasn't a boat on the lake.

As suddenly as it had begun, that summer ended, and for a time we didn't know what to do with ourselves. There were no emergencies. No morning assignments. No muffins to bake. No clattering silverware. Not even any arguments! By Labor Day evening, all the guests had packed up their trailers and cars with their gear and blitzed-out kids, then headed soberly south. Abby was the last to leave, after she'd helped put away the dishes. Zack and the Bees were already back at high school, and Robert was interviewing at a restaurant in Syracuse for a "real job" that would start immediately. In the days that followed, we found things that guests had left behind: a dog-eared paperback, a greasy tube of suntan lotion, a damp bathing suit under a bed. But whose were they? And what should we do with them? They belonged to another time.

So we'd made it, barely, to the off-season. Surely, there was always work to do—it was time to put the summer away—but we could do it at our own speed now. Only on occasional weekends would guests trickle in—the "Leaf Peepers," older folks with trail guides and walking sticks who'd come to see the foliage. It was during that September and October that Fran could again get her fill of "trashy mysteries," as she called them, and I could concentrate on baseball again: Yankee games on the kitchen radio that pulled a wavering signal over the mountains, though only after dark. It was during those months that both sets of our parents returned on separate weekends, so, as they'd agreed, they could each have us all to themselves. Even a few of our teaching friends from Garfield High made the trip, though not Howie this time. Everyone was thrilled that Fran was pregnant, and, perhaps sensing our hard-won satisfaction in living here, kept their thoughts about our "distance from home" mainly under wraps.

It was during those easy-going months that we also had more time to spend with the Wagoners and go to most of the Friday night potluck dinners. In mid-September, we let it be known here that Fran was expecting, and there's nothing like a pregnant woman, especially a *thin* woman, pregnant for the first time, to pluck at the heartstrings and bring out the best in people. Lena Wagoner screamed, weeping with delight at our news, and Bruce lifted me clear off the floor with his big bear hug. Other Year-Rounders dropped by with shopping bags of hand-me-downs and copious advice. Sleep on your left side if you want a girl. Don't swim anywhere around mundungus—as if *anyone* would swim near that stuff.

And it was during that October when Fran got over most of her morning sickness and seemed to enjoy her pregnancy. We both did. You didn't have to look too closely to see that she was showing. Her face was smoother, her neck softer, all her bones, her edges, rounding. She had a calm and determined energy about her. She moved as if pacing herself. She hung the mothballed quilts to air out over the porch railings. She cut back the perennials along the path to the boathouse, while I unhooked all the screens, carried them down to the basement, and, back on the ladder, hooked in the storm windows. On another day I raked the beach, digging up plastic sand toys, and on a warm, Indian summer early-evening, with the sun like a coppery disk, we took a break and took the guide-boat out on the lake.

In case you've never seen or been in one, a guide-boat is a small, light, wooden boat made for carrying, narrow and pointed on each end like a canoe, but like a rowboat, you propel it with oars. It was the vessel of choice in the glory days of the Adirondacks, about 1900, when burly local guides would row New York socialites around the lakes, those wasp-waisted women in corsets and long dresses, with parasols over their shoulders. The guide-boat is a beautiful, delicate, thin-skinned thing, its strakes, or siding planks, only a quarter inch thick and tacked to a skeleton of long, curved ribs, each no bigger around than your finger. It weighs as little as sixty pounds, some significant part of that being its three wicker seats and its layers and layers of varnish. It floats on the water like a shiny, open pod, barely dimpling the surface. In the winters, we keep it winched up in the boathouse, cradled in canvas slings, safely out of the lake. In the warm months, it floats serenely in there, secured on four lines tied to cleats around the edge of the low, narrow dock that forms a little U-shaped bay for the boat. Unlike our scratched and dented aluminum canoes, we rent the guide-boat only to adults. Perfectly balanced and symmetrical, it's the most precious thing we have at the inn.

That evening, Fran and I stepped into the boat, untied the lines from the cleats, and pushed out onto the empty lake. The surface was as calm as I'd ever seen it, a mirror, reflecting the orange maples, along with the greens and yellows along the shore. Seated backwards, I rowed in the front, while Fran, facing me, sat in the wicker seat in the stern, leaning back, her face upturned to the sun. I recall she was wearing a gray sweatshirt of mine and a pair of my corduroy pants with the legs rolled up to her calves, not the look of a New York socialite, not wasp-waisted at all, but she looked awfully good to me. Nor, despite my heavy flannel shirt and jeans, was I the image of a burly Adirondack guide, though I *was*, for the moment at least, feeling downright proud and manly. After all, I was in charge here. I was rowing my wife, my arms going in a comfortable rhythm, pulling us smartly through the water. Moreover, my elegant wardrobe clothed her. And it was me, along with our insect accomplices, who had brought Fran to her state of ripening enlargement.

Anyway, we were gliding along like this, and we were wondering about the sex of this child for about the millionth time. Fran was sure that it was a boy to be called Nat, while I was still holding out for the possibility of a couple of X chromosomes that would grow up to adore her father and go by the name of Natalie. We were in the midst of this enlightening discussion, about a hundred yards away from shore, when Fran's head jerked up and tilted to one side, as if she was listening to something.

I stopped rowing.

She had a puzzled look on her face. Then, involuntarily it seemed, she made a little hiccoughing movement and said, "Whoa!"

"What is it?" I asked.

The boat coasted to a stop.

Then it dawned on her. "He moved!"

"What? Who?"

"The baby!"

"Where?"

"Here, stupid!" She pointed at the middle of her sweatshirt. "Where else do you think he'd move?"

"How do you know?"

"Because I felt it. It's like a fluttering!"

"Well, couldn't it be gas? I mean, there's been a certain abundance of *that*."

She shot me a look and spread her fingers around her stomach. "No. He's glunking around in here! He's swimming!" Her eyes were as wide as I'd ever seen them. She made that weird movement again. "Whoa! Mark, you should feel this!"

I dropped the oars. How could I not? Our child, Nat or Natalie! Its first tiny act of free will! Without thinking, I stood, and, moving toward

Fran, my first step rocked the boat to the right, my next rocked it violently to the left.

"No, I didn't mean that!" she cried. "What are you, nuts? SIT DOWN!"

I tried to, but the seat was swaying, a moving target, and now I was windmilling my arms, trying to keep my balance, everything lurching like crazy. Then it was my turn to yell "Whoa!" and the next thing I knew, I was over the gunwale, for an instant looking up at my boots against the mackerel sky, and then I was in the drink, swimming in my own waters, though they weren't of the warm, amniotic variety.

"You okay?" Fran asked after I came to the surface, hair in my eyes, spitting water. She was still sitting in the wicker seat, her hands bracing her on the gunwale, as the boat rocked more and more gently.

"I'll survive," I said. Which was true. The lake at that time of year, though certainly uncomfortable, hadn't turned frigid yet.

Now the concern on Fran's face gave way to amusement, and she couldn't keep herself from laughing. "Nicely done! Graceful!" she said. "This baby isn't even born, and already he's sent you reeling!"

I swam to the side of the boat, and, using hands and feet, tried to pull myself up and in. But it was one of those things where the more you succeed, the closer you come to failure. It was possible that I might scramble aboard, even in my drenched, leaden clothes, yet only by capsizing the boat and Fran along with it. As she laughed once more, I considered how fitting such an outcome might be, but seeing as there was also an innocent child—a girl!—involved, I decided against it.

Fran crawled to the bow and took the oars. Then with me, her guide, still in the water, shivering and clutching the stern, she rowed us all back toward the boathouse, the blades of the oars, like slow wings, dipping, sweeping, rising, and sweeping. I don't think I'd ever seen her so calm and satisfied, filled with an inner glow that I believe was more than hormonal. She looked at the setting sun, the hills, the lake, and again at me with that smile of hers, just at the corners of her lips. "What a perfect evening," she said, taking a deep breath of the soft, sweet air. "Don't you think?"

8

Though we'd told our parents, the Year-Rounders, and a few friends, we'd yet to inform Mr. Blake and the board of directors that Fran was pregnant. Over the summer, we'd never quite found the time, or rather, we'd never quite gotten up the nerve. Soon, at their annual late-October meeting, they'd be announcing whether they'd renew our contract, and we didn't know how they'd respond to our news, especially after Mr. Blake had received his lapful of our stick-to-the-ribs cooking. But now with Fran all rounding and glowing, there would be no avoiding it. We'd have to tell them.

In the week or so following that afternoon in the guide-boat, some more Leaf Peepers came and went, and I spent much of each day raking up and hauling leaves to the compost heap. We had our first hard frost. I split and laid up wood. Every morning, I set a fire in the living room, and, by midday, it would be toasty inside. At nights, though, we'd slide under the quilt, Fran's stomach against my back, though I never felt the baby moving then. It, too, must have been resting, in sync with Fran, gearing down from the day. How do I describe how good, how "full," to use Fran's term, this felt, the three of us cocooned like that? The salty, tired scent of skin and hair. Fran's rhythmic breath. The gurgling brook. The *whisk* of blown leaves against the window. All so familiar, yet all so new. I seemed to smell, feel, and hear everything then. Often I'd awaken with the faintest *whumph* of the boiler switching on in the basement, and soon I'd hear those tapping and sighing sounds, as the radiators warmed up the dark.

It was close to a year since we'd first come up here for our fateful and triumphant interview. Now again the board members arrived very late after their dinner in Albany, long after we'd gone to bed. Again they assembled the next morning in the dining room. We served coffee, French toast, and fruit cocktail. We left out the grapes. Perhaps because Mr. Dunning was no longer among them, or perhaps because they were all a little older, everyone seemed more subdued this time. Yet something else, like a strained formality, was in the air that we couldn't figure out. No asphyxiating hugs from Beverly Boatwright, no wringing handshakes from Dan Norman. In fact, I had the unnerving impression that they were all avoiding our eyes, while at the same time watching us closely.

Without so much as a salutation, Mr. Blake called the meeting to order. At his suggestion, we observed a moment of silence for Mr. Dunning, "to whom we all owe a great debt of gratitude." Then after Ms. Fringe read the minutes from last year's meeting in a monotone, it was time for our Innkeeper's Report.

Quickly, I summarized our completed and "ongoing"—that is, uncompleted—projects: the warped doors and leaky bathroom faucets, the rooms we'd painted and the many we hadn't, the porch roof that still needed jacking up and bracing, the driveway ruts I'd filled in with gravel that had washed away again and again. . . .

Then Fran stood in her white blouse and olive green jumper that only partially obscured her condition. She passed out copies of bar graphs showing income month by month, and a pie chart showing the distribution of our year-to-date expenses. As always on such occasions, she was focused, energetic, and determinedly optimistic. On balance, the inn was doing okay, she said. Things might even be looking up! In summary, we had more than broken even so far, and it looked like we all might make a little money.

You'd have thought this would cheer the board members, but they remained reserved, their eyes fixed on their placemats. No questions or comments followed Fran's presentation, not even a nod or a "thank you very much."

Irritated, she sat down, and glancing around at those glum, averted faces, I yearned for another Mr. Dunning moment, his silent choking and thrashing string tie. Something to shake things up.

Then, before Mr. Blake could move on to the next agenda item, Fran stood again. Irritation was now exasperation. There was no keeping her down or quiet. This was her damn-the-torpedoes mode, her eyes fiery, her fists on the table, her whole body leaning forward as if to *make* the others lift their chins and say something. By God, she'd wake them up. "As some of you might *see*, if you'd care to *look*," she said, staring at each of them, "Mark and I are expect—"

"Hold it right there!" Mr. Blake cut in, meeting her eyes over his half glasses. "Not another word. Sit down!"

Like a switch turned on, the others came to life, sitting up straight in their chairs.

From his breast pocket, Mr. Blake produced a pink envelope and handed it to me.

I glanced at Fran, and she shrugged her shoulders. What was this all about? If I had to guess, it looked very much like curtains for us. The classic pink slip, with the extra flair of a pink envelope.

"Go on," Mr. Blake said in that same peremptory tone. "Open it."

I did. Inside was a homemade card with a colored drawing on the front of two bird-watchers peering through binoculars at a chubby, winged, pink-looking thing flying toward them over a lake. I studied it closely. Because I'd never seen one with wings, nor seen one in flight like that, it took me a moment to recognize. It was a baby! When I opened the card, it said,

We are thrilled by the prospect!
Congratulations!

Evidently, they had all known our news for some time and had been putting on an act with their grave, indifferent faces, waiting for this moment to come. Below were the signatures of all the board members, followed by a short "P.S.":

> We would very much like you to continue as innkeepers next year, with a salary increase of $500.

Before we could say anything, Mr. Blake asked us when the baby was due. We told him the first week of February, and he said, "All right. I propose that we close the inn for a month beginning the last week of January and reimburse the guests, if any have made reservations. I think we can manage that. You'll both need a break then."

Need I say that the room was filled with relief, joy, hugs, and handshakes? Of course we'd renew our contract!

And need I say that for us the rest of that fall and early winter was a time of nervous anticipation? We cleaned out the little bedroom beside ours in the annex, put a battered bureau beneath the window, and washed down the crib and plastic mattress. With my own hands, I felt the little creature fluttering in Fran's belly, and through Dr. Floyd's stethoscope, we heard a heartbeat. 140 beats per minute! A wild, galloping thing.

Outside on those days, the air was cold, crisp, and smelled of chimney smoke. The frost sifted down every night and clung to the shadows past noon. Except for the pines, the woods had turned gray. The wind whistled through bare branches. Then one evening, we noticed that we hadn't heard the loons. They must have gone as they had come, secretly in the mist or the dark, the same way they moved under water. On another day, we saw wavering skeins of Canada geese, line after line, all heading south and so high that we could barely hear their honking. It seemed that the land, the lake, and the sky were releasing what couldn't persist here. We dressed in long underwear and layers of flannel. We pulled our chairs close to the fire. We were getting down to essentials now, the permanent things, the things that could manage to hold their heat, or the things that were hard and cold.

In the boathouse, I slid the canvas slings under the guide-boat, winched it up out of the water, and put the locking pin through the ratchet. One by one, I carried the rocking chairs from the porch and again stowed them in the basement. Soon the first snow came needling down, ticking on dry leaves, and once from the dock, I saw it actually bouncing on the lake. There comes a time in late November when the water darkens and thickens, seems to change its state, a substance neither liquid nor solid.

Then in the second week of December that year, we had a cold snap, down to five below, and one early morning we saw the first tentative fingers of ice stretching out from the shore in thin sheets. With the midmorning sun, they receded and disappeared. They reappeared the next morning, but when a breeze kicked up, those sheets broke into countless small, gleaming plates, and, floating like shards of glass on the waves, they gently collided and made tinkling sounds, like a million wind chimes going all at once. For about a week, the fingers of ice extended during the night and melted or were shattered by noon. Then on another cold morning, we awoke to see the lake magically knit together, shore to shore, a smooth, black, shiny skin, studded with feathery "frost flowers" we called them, like tiny cotton balls. The open water was gone. A breeze didn't ruffle the glazed surface, and the sun didn't melt it. From then until spring, the lake would be frozen, intractable, a vast, silent presence, the ice gaining strength by reaching down and thickening.

When, for years, you've been trying to conceive a child—and especially when you're actually doing it—you're not much focused on the tail end of the process, the how, when, and in what sort of interesting circumstances a child might eventually be born. These eventualities, though, have a way of catching up with you.

About the time of the freeze-up, we began our six weekly childbirth classes at Memorial Hospital in Amsterdam, about fifty miles south down Route 30. With four other couples, whose average ages were approximately seventeen, we learned all about the wonderful stages of labor: latent, active, and, best of all, advanced or transitional labor. We learned about such delicacies as the "mucous plug" and the "bloody show." We toured the maternity floor and the white-tiled delivery rooms, and beheld all the fancy cutlery. With a registered nurse wearing long braids and with another, intensely calm and silent woman who sat before us like the Buddha, we practiced relaxation and breathing techniques that left neither of us particularly relaxed and Fran completely out of breath, blue in the face, and panting like a retriever. I learned that through the arduous journey of childbirth, I was to be Fran's "coach," guiding, encouraging, and soothing her. In the labor room, I would stroke her abdomen and massage her back. I'd hold her hand when it trembled. During active and advanced labor, I'd drape cool washcloths over her forehead and slide warm socks on her feet. On the portable tape deck, I might play soft music, possibly Gregorian chants. I'd slide ice chips between her parched lips. I'd "breathe her over" the worst contractions and help her recover between them. Together, we'd banish fear and dramatically reduce the "perception of pain." Above all, I'd be supportive, reassuring, and in words that don't often come to me when I think of myself: steady and level-headed.

By mid-December, we usually have a foot or two of snow, and as it started piling up that winter, the first weekend cross-country skiers arrived in their down vests, parkas, and swishing snow pants—they looked like walking sleeping bags. For those Saturdays and Sundays, we rehired the trusty Killer Bees to help us in the dining room and kitchen. Then at Christmas, Fran's parents came up from New Jersey. We read the Bible story before we opened presents.

"I don't get it," Fran said, when I'd closed the book. "I mean, one second Mary's 'great with child,' then, bingo, she 'brings him forth,' and voilà!—he's all clean, pink-cheeked, wrapped in swaddling cloths and shimmering with light. Mary doesn't even break a sweat! How come she had it so easy?"

"Maybe she had no perception of pain," I said, "because she had such a good coach."

"Joseph? He wasn't even up the brook with Mary! Why would he hang around the delivery room? He was useless. By the way, *our* coach has plowed the driveway, right?"

For Christmas gifts, we all went utilitarian that year. Fran's parents, buoyant with the idea of their first grandchild, gave us an entire "layette," a noun I'd never heard before, meaning a stockpile of tiny undershirts, diapers, pins, plastic pants, sweaters, bibs, receiving blankets, and funny, stretchy pajama things with feet in them. I gave Fran a kid's wooden highchair which I'd found in pieces down in the basement. Following the instructions in a woodworking manual, I'd secretly glued it back to together, stripped off the old cracked paint, sanded it, brushed on a couple coats of urethane, and I don't mind saying that it looked pretty good, a solid piece of furniture, when I brought it upstairs and set it on the hearth in front of Fran with a big red bow on the seat.

"Mark! *You* did *that*?" she asked, astonished and with a little catch in her voice.

Then she gave me a new pair of insulated work gloves and an aluminum-framed kid-carrying backpack which she'd bought at the Wagoner's garage sale. "Now we can *both* do some heavy lifting," she said.

"I'm ready," I replied.

And I was. We were both ready. We were more than ready. This pregnancy, while filling us with hope and excitement, was also getting a little old by then, and we were still six weeks from the due date. Those cute flutterings in Fran's belly had become judo kicks to her ribs. About every half hour, she had to wobble to the bathroom, and just turning over in bed involved much loud hoisting, torqueing, and strategic repositioning of a half-dozen pillows. Her legs were now mapped with veins. Her back ached. Her belly looked explosive. While certain big-boned women seem to *absorb* a pregnancy, Fran was a wisp with a bowling ball out front. "Look out below!" she'd say, coming down the annex stairs to the kitchen. Or climbing up, breathless: "Get me the winch, would you?"

Miraculously, we got through the early-January Elks Club dinner without any egregious mistakes, and mercifully we finished up our birth classes. Then Fran began her more frequent, weekly appointments with Dr. Floyd, and soon we filled up a small suitcase to take to the hospital, a "go bag," which waited beside the door like a sprinter in the blocks. It amuses me to think how carefully we packed it, checking off each item on our list, as if we could impose some order on the event we were anticipating. The watch with the sweep second hand for timing contractions. The cassette player, extra batteries, and tapes. Powders, lotions, lip balm, granola bars, washcloths, rag socks, and—get this!—a rolling pin to massage Fran's back. What sort of weird outing was this?

By mid-month, the fishing shanties had all reappeared on the lake, though on many days the snow whirled down in veils so thick that you couldn't even see the boathouse. On the knoll, the wind whipped drifts into corniced waves and moving, fingering dunes. They swallowed shrubs. They lapped over the porch. Religiously, I kept the van topped up with gas. I plowed and shoveled to keep the path, the parking lot, and the driveway open for our quick getaway to the hospital.

With February came those first very occasional and mild contractions—Braxton Hicks contractions, they're called—that Dr. Floyd said we shouldn't worry about. A few days later, Fran said she could actually feel the baby "drop," moving lower into position. We waited and waited. I plowed and shoveled. The snow banks around the parking lot mounded up. The path was a tunnel to the van. Nightly, we got calls from the Wagoners or our parents. "How're you doing? Just checking in. Anything, you know, going on?" By day, Fran would have short rushes of Herculean energy, wielding sponges, buckets, and the array of vacuum attachments, "deep cleaning" the entire annex. Then, exhausted, she'd sit for hours looking at the lake through the living room window. Dr. Floyd said "soon," but still nothing happened. Except that it snowed and snowed.

In the end, however, it wasn't the snow that got us. On the night that Fran's real contractions started, we were in for a change of plans. Naturally, it was one in the morning.

"Guess what," she said gently, waking me.

I shot bolt upright in bed, adrenaline pumping, prepared as I was for this moment. "This is it! Right? Ready? Let's go!"

Evidently, she'd been lying there, awake and silent for some time. She said yes, this was it and she was ready, but she didn't move, then added mysteriously, "I'm not sure we're going anywhere."

I fumbled for and pushed the switch on my lamp, but it didn't go on. On hands and knees, I scrambled on the floor and found the flashlight beneath the bedside table. I picked up the phone on the bureau to call the hospital, but the line was dead. I put down the receiver. "I can't get through!"

"Shhh." She didn't seem particularly surprised or upset. "Stop for a second and listen."

I stopped and listened. Without noticing it, I'd been hearing it all along: a low drumming, usually a soothing sound, something commonplace yet strange. "It's raining! In the middle of winter, it's raining!"

I went to the window and, parting the curtains, pointed the flashlight into the darkness. In the cone of light that reached into the woods, every branch, twig, and bough drooped and gleamed like crystal, each glazed with a half inch of ice. A puff of wind made the drumming harder, and from outside I could hear cracking and shattering sounds. Finally, it dawned on me: this could complicate matters.

On my bureau, I've always kept a battery-powered radio tuned to the twenty-four hour weather service and emergency channel from Glens Falls. I turned it on, and we learned that a stalled low pressure system mixing arctic and unexpectedly warm Gulf air had produced ice storms in a two hundred mile swath from Binghamton to St. John. All the

Adirondacks were dark. Trunk lines down. Steel transmission towers collapsed. Niagara-Mohawk was overwhelmed. The Northway had closed, the Thruway too, all the way from Rochester to Catskill. Fallen trees and phone poles crisscrossed state highways, and God help the smaller roads. Nothing was moving anywhere.

"Looks like we're here for a while," Fran said in that same tone, as she heaved her legs over the side of the bed. She waved off a helping hand from me and pushed herself upright. "Think I'll take a quick shower, if the water's still hot."

I gave her the flashlight. In my bureau drawer, there was another, which, after I'd dressed, I took outside toward the garage on my way to get the generator going, something I'd finally learned how to do. Everything out there was darkly glazed and shining. I could barely stand. All around, the rain made a metallic pinging. Huge limbs, like arches, bent to the ground. Ice encased our van in the lot, and, as if felled by a cleaver, a maple had split, half of it across the driveway.

Back in the inn, at the fuse box in the basement, I switched off all the circuits, except the ones for the annex and the kitchen. I had gone back upstairs and turned on a few lights, when Fran came out of the bathroom in slippers and a fresh nightgown. She was huge, which made her arms look like pencils. She smelled clean, like Ivory soap. Her hair was wet, straight, and combed back neatly behind her ears. She still seemed oddly calm.

"Well, at least I won't do this in a manger," she said. "There's plenty of room at *this* inn." We went downstairs, where I made a cup of tea in the kitchen as Fran walked around in the other rooms, the floorboards creaking. When she stopped, I could hear her touching and moving a side table or chair, as if to get things in order. In the dim light, she lay down on the sofa. She didn't even want a sip of tea, and in a while she was twitching and fidgeting. She couldn't make herself comfortable, and over the next couple hours, as the contractions got worse and more frequent, neither of us was calm any more.

Too frantically, I tried to do what I was supposed to do. When Fran was hot, I put damp washcloths over her forehead, but they were too cold.

"I'm freezing!"

So I slid wool socks on her feet.

"I'm boiling!" And she kicked them off.

I fed her slivers of ice. I lit a candle on the end table. I played soothing music on the tape deck from the go bag. But it was all so incidental. None of it mattered. None of it, as was said in our birth class, could "give a sense of control."

With the pain, Fran's eyes drifted away. For long periods, she was somewhere else, groaning and rocking, while the icy rain beat on the windows.

Sometime later—I'm not sure how long—she got off the sofa and started groping desperately toward the kitchen, her hands moving like birds on the walls and moldings. She wouldn't let me touch her. She told me to push the kitchen table into the corner, between the stove and some boxes of canned peaches. She told me to get pillows, towels, and blankets, and spread them under the table—which I did. Then, like a kid getting into a make-believe fort, or an animal settling into a makeshift den, she bent low and crawled under.

"This can't be the most sanitary situation," I said. "And isn't there a more comfortable place?"

"No!"

It seemed like the most ridiculous question, but I asked, "Can I come in?"

"Well, I can't stop you," she said, which wasn't exactly a warm invitation, but I crawled in anyhow.

So then we were both under the table, in a weird little hut in the corner of the kitchen in an ice storm in the middle of the Adirondacks, with neither of us in the most steady of moods, trying to have a baby.

I crouched beside her. When the contractions came almost continuously, like hammer blows, she sunk her fingernails into my palms.

At one point, exhausted, she said, "That's it. I'm done. I'm taking my things and going home!"

At another point, when she was writhing with back labor, her legs shaking, her face clenched, I tried to be calm, to reassure her. "Everything's going to be okay."

But she'd have none of it. "You think *this* looks okay?"

"But we're making progress."

"*We*? Did I hear you say *we*?!"

"Look, I'm trying to help!"

"Well, for God's sake, then do something!"

"I've been trying!" Now *I* was losing it. "But every time I try, you go ballistic!" Evidently, at this nativity, I was even *worse* than Joseph. A hindrance!

Fran started sobbing and screaming all at once. I was screaming too. And you might imagine how she responded when I offered to get the rolling pin. It wasn't our finest hour.

Now there came another period when she drifted off, which ended when she opened her eyes and announced matter-of-factly, "All right. I'm getting this over with. It's time."

She sat up against the pillows and soon was focusing everything that was in her, bearing down, pushing, grunting, gritting her teeth, veins popping on her forehead. There was blood, fluid, and heat everywhere. Everything smelled like the sea. Fran seemed to be pounding, mashing down the baby. The bulge in her stomach stretched, flattened, and I remember yelling, "This is ridiculous! You're beating each other to pulps!"

But she didn't even hear me. She kept on pounding. . . .

And then into my hands came the weirdest thing: a grapefruit-sized head, slick as an otter, soft as a ripe avocado.

And there was an ear, a tiny shell.

Then a shoulder, a bluish, bony knob.

Then the other shoulder.

And then, Jesus, the whole rest of her. Yes, it was *her*. Long arms, little fists, round torso, narrow hips, legs, wrinkled knees and splayed toes came wriggling and sliding, blotchy, bloody, pink, with cheesy stuff in the folds of her skin, and trailing the twisted purple cord, thick as BX cable.

And then I had all of her, a live little animal.

Then she let out a wild, angry howl.

Then I gave her to Fran, who wrapped her in her arms.

Then I made a tourniquet with twine and cut the cord with the bread knife.

Then I threw blankets and blankets over them. I couldn't hear the rain anymore. "Natalie," I said when I could say anything.

And weeping and trembling, Fran cried, "Natalie! Yes, Natalie. Of course!" Then, even then, she shot me that dig-in-the-heels look that was pure Fran. "But for short we'll call her . . . Nat."

10

So you go through all this. You fret for years that you're incomplete. You fight, love, and mate like cats. Then, amazingly, it happens. You set in motion an unwieldy and dangerous process, and when it comes to its harrowing and exhilarating end, you have in your hands the most strange, messy, needy, demanding, and, to be honest, not the most beautiful creature on the face of the earth.

But Nat was healthy, and Fran, though wiped out, would be okay, as we learned from Dr. Floyd the following morning, after I'd chain sawed and cleared the elm limbs from the driveway, and the county trucks had spread sand on the icy road. If he'd known of our circumstances, I'm sure Dr. Floyd would've made his way to the inn, but as the phones were still dead, we had no way of getting in touch with him.

"You've just delivered this child *at home*?" he asked, incredulous, as we staggered into the clinic with Nat in Fran's arms, and both of them wrapped in blankets.

Unfortunately, he'd addressed this question to me, which would have roused Fran even from her deathbed. "I believe I had *some* part in it!" she said with the glint of a blade in her eye.

When I said that Nat was otter-like when she was born, I wasn't kidding. Her head was elongated as if for tunneling, her fingers, with those sharp little nails, like claws for digging into muddy banks. Her whole body seemed sleeked for parting waters, and this really got me: for the first four or five days, the kid was hairy, or furry, and not just on the top of her head, but in places where I thought only animals and certain football players were hairy, across her back and upper arms.

Still, we said, and absolutely meant, that she was the most precious thing. All of our desperate wanting had turned into desperate love and ferocious, anxious caring. When Nat cried inconsolably in the middle of the night, Fran tried one breast, then the other. For the hundredth time,

I changed Nat's diaper, buttering her with A&D ointment and showering her with baby powder. We sang lullabies. In midnight phone calls to the Wagoners, we sought reassurance and counsel. We sang Springsteen's "Born to Run." I walked Nat all around the inn, switching her from arms to shoulder to arms again. Back upstairs, we laid her in the crib with pillows all around. We rubbed her back. We wound up the little lamb with a music box in its bowels. Once I brought in the radio and turned on the twenty-four hour weather service, which at least caught Nat's attention. Maybe, already, she was a child of the Adirondacks. Maybe wind speeds, dew points, and snow accumulations would take her mind off whatever was bugging her, would ease her off into sleep.

No way! She cried and cried, thrashing her arms and legs, her hands clenched, her face beet-red. Gas? Colic? We were frantic. We were zombies for that first month, exhausted, even when Fran's mother came and helped for a week, and it wasn't until one particularly bad night, when I saw Fran's bottom bureau drawer wide open, that I had a brilliant, faintly murderous idea. I laid Nat in the drawer and started pushing it closed. That would at least muffle the din.

"What in the world are you doing?" Fran yelled.

"Shh," I said. "Listen."

As I slowly pushed, Nat's crying softened, until she mewed like a kitten. By the time the drawer was only open a couple of inches, she was silent and sleeping, curled in that dark little den among Fran's socks and underwear.

Of course, on the following weekend, when my parents came to see their own first grandchild, my mother was horrified when she saw this. "It looks like the poor child's in a casket!" she said, not mincing her words, and rushed off to Albany to buy a fancy, white basinet which Nat refused to sleep in. So back into the bureau drawer went our burrowing baby, where she slept peacefully for the first nine months of her life, a second gestation, until she couldn't fit in there anymore.

Come to think of it, Nat, as a child, would always like tight, protected spaces, as if the world was too wide and bright to easily step into. As a toddler, she didn't really toddle that much, exploring and getting into things, but preferred to be swaddled deep in that kid-carrying pack that, for a couple years, seemed attached to my shoulders and hips. She was squinty, hesitant, and afraid of strangers, not exactly the optimum psychological profile for the child of innkeepers.

Even in our photos of her as a two- and three-year-old among other children, she was never in the center but usually on the edges of things, off in the background at her own birthday parties, her thin arms squeezed to her sides, her hands clasped behind her back, a kid who preferred the shadows. In preschool, at "circle time," she wasn't overtly unhappy or unfriendly, just very reserved and quiet. In kindergarten, her teacher described her as "inward," "dreamy," and "withdrawn." In the little storage area in the back of her closet, beneath the sloped roof and above the eaves, she'd amuse herself for hours, often with her imaginary friends or with her miniature plastic animals arranged in perfect rows on the floor. She never liked to go out on the swing. It was always "too scary."

I can see now that at least in part, Nat was molded by—and molded herself in response to—her surroundings, which were not very well suited to her. She lived in a country inn a half hour from the nearest village, on a dirt road three miles from the intersection on Route 8, where Fran or I would wait with her in the van until the school bus came and she'd reluctantly climb aboard. Then she'd sit alone in the very back, looking downward as the bus pulled away. She didn't fit in with the more hardscrabble, brawny, rough-and-tumble kids in the local elementary school. When we invited some of them over, Nat didn't want to play tag or "King of the Hill." She was always small and short for her age. Like Fran and me, she was built like a stick, and on her chest and at her temples, you could see her spidery blue veins, her skin translucent and delicate as a petal. To me, she always seemed so *pervious.*

Nor, as a seven-, eight-, and nine-year-old, did she fit in with the confident, boisterous children who visited the inn on their family vacations and who were more sophisticated in a downstate, suburban mall sort of way, their currency being movies, sports, and clothes that we couldn't have afforded, even if they were available up here. Moreover, on those rare occasions when Nat *did* strike up a fledgling friendship, say, with a fellow third-grade girl in room #4, that friend would disappear two weeks later. *"Daddy, where did she go? She was so nice. I didn't even have a chance to say goodbye."* No wonder Nat kept mainly to herself.

Like I've said, we loved her ferociously—but in different ways. In a reversal of our habits as high school teachers, as parents I was all heat and kinetic energy, while Fran was more calm. When Nat and I were together and there was silence between us, I'd always fill it with chatter. Fran's ministries, on the other hand, were more subtle and effective. A current ran between her and Nat that was deeper than anything I could understand. Fran's way with Nat was to be quietly and sympathetically available. She'd busy herself washing windows in the kitchen, as Nat, in fifth or sixth grade, would wrestle at the table with her homework or recount those slights and disappointments that always seemed to come her way: "Why wasn't I invited to the birthday party? Why am I never chosen for the team?"

"Sometimes things don't make any sense," I'd say, overhearing her as I came into the kitchen. "Sometimes it's just bad luck."

Fran would look at Nat with her heart in her eyes. She'd start to say something, but then abruptly stop, sensing that words only went so far, and she'd take Nat into her arms.

As I think of all this, as I try to piece together some picture of Nat's childhood, I realize that I still haven't gotten it right, or as close to right as I'd like. It's true that she was quiet, uncertain, and frequently alone. But it's also true that Nat found some things in her aloneness that sustained her, some pleasures that Fran and I would appreciate, even as Nat held them closely to herself and we often just saw them in glimpses.

When she was eleven, I taught Nat how to use the guide-boat, a special privilege for a kid her age, and, surprising to me, she really took to it, perhaps because it was solitary. I showed her how, crouching, to step into the boat from the dock inside the boathouse, how to untie the lines from the cleats and push out onto the lake. I showed her how to launch from the beach in shallow water, putting a hand on each gunwale and one foot in the stern, and then, with the other foot, shoving off and swinging aboard, a technique that took me years to learn by trial and mostly error. But after only a few wet, determined attempts, Nat got the hang of it. "I did it!" she said, delighted with herself. And she kept doing it and doing it, pushing the boat out, swinging aboard, and with a couple of quick, careful steps, sitting down in the middle seat. She also got the hang of rowing cross-handed without mashing her fists together where the oar handles overlapped. And she learned how to set a course by sighting a landmark above the stern, and that your straightest way forward when rowing a guide-boat is to keep your eyes looking back.

On calm summer afternoons, she'd row out on the lake in her orange life jacket. She'd set off in one direction, keeping a straight line. Then, in what must have been a different mood, she'd let go of the oars that are fixed to their pins. Lying down in the boat, she'd just drift out there, probably watching the clouds, as I'd putter in the boathouse or on the beach, keeping her in sight.

What pleased Nat the most, however, was swimming. Even better than being *on* the lake was being *in* it. She was transformed by water. Awkward and timid on land, she swam with surprising ease and power, with long, steady strokes. She'd dive under the surface and weave like an eel. She could tread water forever. I recall how Fran showed her how to do the crawl. Nat must have been only four or five years old back then, in a rainbow-colored bathing suit. They were both standing in the lake, beside the boathouse, where the water came up over Nat's waist.

"Make your hands into cups and do this," Fran said. Alternately, she reached out her arms, then, rotating, drew them toward her, reaching out again and again. "Imagine you're pulling the lake toward you. Kick your feet and breathe like this." Fran turned her head to the right and took a breath as she cocked her arm on that side. Then to further demonstrate, she took a few steps into deeper water and dove in, swimming deliberately, her elbows high and her long legs fluttering, boiling the water behind her.

Perhaps thirty feet out there, she turned around and was swimming back, when, without any encouragement or warning, Nat just threw herself toward Fran, sinking for a scary moment, then coming up with her arms churning and feet kicking. Desperate but making progress, she swam in Fran's direction, like this was something she'd always known but hadn't discovered yet.

"She's a fish!" Fran called to me where I stood on the beach, as Nat, exhilarated, arrived in her arms.

"I can swim!" Nat cried.

And my God, could she! Within three or four weeks—and in her life jacket then—she was doing the sidestroke and, her favorite, the backstroke. Even with her eyes fixed on the sky, she seemed to know where she was going. Every summer thereafter for a number of years, she'd be the first to dive off the dock in mid-June, weeks before the summer guests arrived, when the water was still bitterly cold. In early October, she'd be the last to step out of the lake, sometimes with bright leaves stuck to her skin like ornaments. Almost always, as Fran or I watched from the beach, she preferred to swim alone, and, as she got older, she'd swim out toward the middle, a dot in all that flatness. Other times, nearer the shore, she'd float and frolic, somersaulting underwater, surfacing and diving like a porpoise, all for the pure pleasure of it.

I'll never forget seeing her out there, that sense of how different and apart we were. Then a few times, even as I felt that difference, I'd be surprised by the opposite feeling. Eventually, Nat would swim toward the beach, stand up, streaming in the shallow water, then run up on the sand where I'd hold out a towel like a bullfighter. This was near the end of those middle years, before Nat was a teenager, when she was still no higher than my chest, and there were moments when we could be easy and unself-conscious with one another. Hugging herself and saying *brrrrrrrrr* with her blue lips, she'd sprint into the towel. I'd wrap it around her, feeling all her shivering aliveness. And mine. Her body thrummed like a tuning fork. She was so happy then. *Snug as a bug in a rug.* With my arms under her knees and back, I'd lift and carry her across the sand, smelling the lake in her hair. She'd hold on with an arm around my neck. I'd feel her relax and go lanky, her legs dangling like wind chimes. Comfort was something we could give each other then, even if only for moments. I'd take her to the dock that was drenched in sun, and lay her down on the warm boards.

During all those years, Fran and I continued to keep the inn—or we were supposed to. In the hectic months, as always, we were running around with our hair on fire, trying to do too many things. Each summer our staff was a new and challenging assortment of talent. Other generations of ditzy girls replaced the Killer Bees. Zack stayed on for a couple of summers before we hired a born again Baptist, the most polite teenager known to man, though he didn't work on Sundays. Then some time in there, we finally entered the age of technology. We bought a phone message machine and put our revenue, expenses, and taxes all on computer, though we *still* don't have reliable cell phone service in this area. We hired a company in Syracuse to design a website where guests could make reservations online, as well as by email. Each year Abby, who'd been briefly married and continued moving from job to job, helped (that is, *saved*) us at some crucial point during the summer—she just couldn't relax and "vacation" here. Each year we earned barely enough to keep ourselves and the inn afloat and Mr. Blake and board of directors more or less appeased. Each year they renewed our contract, sometimes with a little raise in salary. Without knowing it, we'd achieved a wobbly equilibrium where we fixed things up almost as fast as other things fell apart.

Yes, we did *think* about having another child, a sibling for Nat, but perhaps because Fran and I had been only children ourselves, a larger family didn't feel imperative. We never tried to get pregnant again. All the charts and thermometers. All that trouble. And what with innkeeping and occasionally visiting our parents, who had retired and were living in condos back in Jersey—and most of all with caring for Nat—we had enough on our plates already.

As for our social lives, in the off seasons, we still got together with our friends, the Wagoners, whose kids were in high school or had grown up and left home, and with whom we played cards, talked for hours, and occasionally saw year-old "just released" movies at the tiny theater in Speculator. At some point, we must have qualified as Year-Rounders, or *adopted* Year-Rounders, and I suppose I first realized this during one of those potluck dinners at Orma's, when Fran and I would come armed with a casserole and some gossip about our guests. On that particular night, Wes Magoon, sitting next to Fran, was telling some humorous story after dessert, when he started having trouble enunciating his words. He stopped and said, "Damn, these things!" Then he pulled out his teeth, upper and lower plates, and set them, wet and glistening, on the table beside Fran's arm, and went right on with his story. No one said a word or even seemed to notice this, though I do remember Fran turning her head slightly toward me, her eyebrows going up, and giving me her quick, bemused look that said, *Well, I guess we're all on pretty familiar terms here.*

Meanwhile, Nat struggled through junior high and her freshman year in high school at the big, central school in Wells, twenty miles away, where all her peers charged mercilessly into adolescence. Pierced ears. Lipstick. Widening hips. Rounding breasts. All that preening and parading. And there she was, so slow to develop, still straight and plain as a two-by-four, still with that pale, translucent skin, and her face so wary and watchful: *Why isn't anyone interested in me? What's wrong?*

But then, eventually, came her sophomore year, when everything—and I mean *everything*!—changed so fast that I could barely take it all in. Though in theory, I knew it was coming, I was still blindsided, stunned. As if to make up for lost time, Nat must have grown four inches in as many months, her body lengthening, curving and softening, still narrow, but attractive in a willowy, pliant way, so suddenly a vibrant sexual being—and she knew it. She was different. She even smelled different, that sharp, alive, teenage scent. What I had taught to hundreds of students in Health back at Garfield High, I couldn't possibly say to my own daughter. So it was Fran who huddled with Nat behind her closed bedroom door and who took her on those secret trips to the pharmacy section of the grocery store to pick up "feminine supplies." Soon small, shallow bras mushroomed up in the laundry basket. Pink "Lady Schick" shavers appeared on the shelf in the shower, joined by an arsenal of plastic bottles of foam, gel, and spray. Tubes of acne salve multiplied in the bathroom cupboard, while in the medicine cabinet, a new pile of sheathed tampons, stacked like cordwood, crowded out my razor.

It was shortly after that, in the spring of 2003, when Nat, our shy little girl, who was born under a table, had slept in a drawer, and played in that small storage area in the back of her closet, leapt headlong out of the shadows. At the time, Fran and I could hardly believe it. No reassuring books and articles on teenage development and behavior could have prepared us, not when it was happening to Nat. Overnight, her childhood had ended, and unlike Fran and me, she didn't mourn its passing for a second. She seemed to revolt against it, or against herself. She was sixteen, going on twenty. She spent an eternity in front of the bathroom mirror. She made friends with girls who, by the looks of their skimpy outfits, were not the most healthy or inspiring peer group. One afternoon she came home from a friend's wearing eyeliner. On another, her eyebrows had vanished. On yet another, her perfectly good jeans seemed to have gone through a shredder, revealing through various artful slashes glimpses of calves, thighs, and even the lacy black edge of some panties that I'd never seen in the wash. When she went swimming that summer, it wasn't here but at "swim parties" over at Lake Pleasant. "Why? Because that's where everyone *is*!" she informed Fran and me, as though we hadn't a brain in our heads.

As a junior, she grew her reddish-brown hair long and thick as a mane, and walked so it swayed across her back. I remember this because, in any public place, even at the market over in Speculator, she'd speed up and, as if we were strangers, walk a few strides ahead of me now, jeans swishing, hair swaying, head turning quick as a bird's, scanning the aisles for signs of teenage life.

In the annex one evening, I found her draped across the sofa again, too tired to lift a finger. She was wearing an oversized T-shirt that I didn't recognize. Her stuff was strewn all over the place, like at a rummage sale.

"When you have some energy, could you clean up your things?" I said. "And your room, too. It's a disaster area."

She looked at me, astounded, as if I'd asked her to run a marathon.

Then the phone rang, and—bang!—she jumped up, bolted across our living area, grabbed the receiver before anyone else, and clamped it between her ear and shoulder. "Hey!"

She took the phone into her bedroom so she could talk in private. I heard whispers, a low, conspiratorial tone, and with a sinking heart, I knew: boys. Maybe even senior boys or boys who had graduated. Meaty guys with thumbs hooked in front pockets, with licenses and cars with wide back seats and six-packs of Genny Cream on the floor. Or pot in the glove box?

From the high school counselor, Fran and I had learned what we already suspected, and more: "She's a good kid, but she's testing the limits. She's come into school late a few times, not on the bus. And while I'm pretty sure she's not directly involved, recently she's been hanging around some questionable characters, kids far more daring than she is. Drugs and such. You'll have to set clear boundaries."

"Who was that?" I asked Nat when she finished on the phone and came out of her room—about an hour after she'd gone in there.

"Nobody," she said breezily. "Nobody to get worked up about." Then she turned and flew down the stairs, legs and ankles thin as a fawn's, all that hair bouncing behind her.

11

"Nobody," of course, turned out to be somebody. Or somebodies. And one of those somebodies during that late summer after Nat's junior year was a guy named Chuck Frazier, the son of Ted and Clara Frazier, who were long-time Regulars, though this would be their last time here, as they were coming up in the world and would soon go on fancier vacations. A few summers before, Chuck had been "Charlie," just another spindly, curly-headed kid who ran on the beach and threw a Frisbee for hours. Now he was tall, had ropey muscles, a deep tan, stubble on his face, and hair under his arms, and his curls had grown into long, blonde waves that put you in mind of surfers. When he was wearing any sort of shirt at all, he wore a blue college sweatshirt. He also wore a backwards baseball cap that said "Just Do It!" and he walked in a cocky, loose-jointed way that made you wonder how his baggy swimming shorts ever stayed on his narrow hips. He must have been at least eighteen because, during the two weeks his family was here on vacation, he drove his parents' new silver BMW, churning in and out of the driveway, spitting stones, and churning Fran's and my insides, as well. He'd always been a fun-loving, daredevil kid with an infectious smile, who in his early teens had learned how to slalom water ski, how to lean way back, carving through the water at breakneck speed, once wearing one of his father's red business ties, and to tell the truth, I'd always liked him, though things would get more complicated.

I don't know exactly when he and Nat first caught each other's eye as blossoming teenagers, but that August you couldn't help but feel the attraction, like a charge in the air. He was just so hungry, self-assured, and handsome in his lean and casual way. And she was just so curious, eager, ready and not ready for anything.

During his initial days here that summer, he and Nat would loosely drift around one another, he, in his sweatshirt, hanging around the inn, suddenly interested in the landscape photos on the living room walls or the contents of the bookshelves. Or she, in her jeans, flip-flops, and tank top—and suddenly interested in things automotive—would wander over to the parking lot, where he'd be fiddling with that car, bent over the engine or waxing the hood, a sheen of sweat on his back and shoulders.

As advised, Fran and I tried to set boundaries. We said that Nat had to be in every night by ten. We said that under no circumstances could she go out driving with Chuck behind the wheel. So cleverly, in the evenings, they'd sit for hours, low down in the front seats of that BMW, parked in the back corner of the lot. I guess that's the thing about living in the wilderness. What boundaries there are you can wriggle around, and so much is unrestricted or indefinite. You won't find many fences or walls around here. We seldom speak of property as "lots." One thing blends into another. By degrees, a gravel road becomes a dirt road, which narrows down to an old wagon track, which becomes a foot trail, which peters out into a deer path overhung with foliage . . . and then you're just into the thick of it, "bushwhacking."

Over the next week, we saw less and less of Nat. With Chuck, she was always down on the beach, or out somewhere on a long walk, or transfixed by the beauty of a V-8, 324-horsepower engine. When she was here, she was usually "busy" in her room, with her music going behind her closed door late into the night. In the mornings, she slept later and later, often missing breakfast altogether. When occasionally she couldn't avoid us, she was certainly uninterested in our interest in and concern for her. "Back off!" she said. In the kitchen, she'd leave a carton of ice cream on the stove top and put silverware away in the refrigerator. Once I saw her rinsing the same coffee cup for minutes on end, and she jumped when, without meaning to, I disturbed her. Her whole being was elsewhere.

Then on the night before the Saturday when Chuck and his parents were to leave, she didn't come home by ten. Nor by ten-thirty, when Fran and I usually said goodnight to the guests remaining in the living room and headed up to bed. Nor even by eleven. Nor had she called from wherever she was to say she was late. Sheepishly, we knocked on the Fraziers' door and asked Ted and Clara if they knew of Chuck's whereabouts. We said he "might" be out somewhere with Nat.

Older, and perhaps because he was a guy, Chuck was on a looser leash than she. "Oh, if they're out somewhere, they'll turn up soon," Ted said offhandedly. "Kids," he added by way of explanation, which, for Fran and me, wasn't explanation enough.

So I took the flashlight outside where the wind was kicking up. Near the parking lot, I cringed with visions of what I might see or interrupt. Did I really want to find them? No. But not finding them would be even worse.

There in the back corner was the BMW, crouching on its wide tires, but no one was inside. I went down to the beach and shined the flashlight across the sand, all bumped and dented with footprints. Here and there, I saw a plastic shovel or a castle some kids had made. Canoes lay upside down, like strange, misplaced bananas. On the far end of the beach, a small campfire danced in the wind and darkness, and, walking over, I said a few words to the circle of folks who were just breaking up before heading to the inn for bed. None of them had seen Nat or Chuck that evening. Retracing my steps, I shined the flashlight on the shaggy field where the tall grasses were swaying and thrashing. I turned off the light and for a while stood still and listened. I heard waves breaking on the beach, and people laughing and saying goodnight, after they'd doused the campfire. It was one of those times when a cool westerly wind carries the smell of the lake mixed with pine and that sudden sense that these late summer nights are so few and fleeting, going, almost gone, as you live them.

I turned the flashlight back on and, following some intuition, crossed the sand toward the boathouse, a dark, peaked, boxy shape, with its hip roof overhanging much of the dock that extends a good ways into the water. I went up the granite step to the paint-chipped back door, then lifted the latch and followed the beam of my flashlight inside. The air in the boathouse smelled of waterlogged wood and the muddy nests of barn swallows. To my left were the empty canoe racks and the warped stairs that lead through a trap door to the storage attic above, which was still padlocked. *No, they couldn't be up there.* Straight ahead, ropes and pulleys hung from beams. To my right and attached to a thick post was the winch for hauling up the guide-boat for the winter. There were the life jackets hanging from pegs on the wall. There on the narrow dock were the horn-shaped cleats to which the boat should have been tied. But the bay between the docks was empty, and near the middle of one dock lay Nat's flip-flops and Chuck's blue sweatshirt in a heap, alongside four empty beer bottles.

I went back out the door, around the corner of the boathouse and walked to the end of the dock. Again, I listened and waited. No stars, no moon. Out there, the wind seemed stronger, flapping my sleeves and making me squint. I swept the flashlight across the lake, where for twenty yards I could see the rolling waves, some with white caps, and then the light seemed to die on its vastness. *That boat, with its low freeboard, wasn't made for these waves. What are they doing out there?*

I went back to the inn where all the guests had retired, and pulled the door to the porch closed—no one locks up around here. I switched off the lamps, except for the one by the picture window. I left another lamp lit on the kitchen table, then went up the annex stairs and sat on the sofa with Fran. She was in her terrycloth bathrobe, dead tired, her eyes pouched, her feet curled beneath her, but like me, not ready for sleep.

I told her what I'd found and hadn't found in the boathouse. "Nat and Chuck, they must be out on the lake somewhere."

"In the pitch dark? In the wind? What if they capsize?"

"Well, if they're sober, they could probably swim to shore."

"But doesn't that depend on where they are? It's a big lake, Mark."

I gave her a look. "You don't have to tell me that."

"So what do we do?"

"What *can* we do? We wait. Nat knows how to handle the boat. Maybe they've holed up on the island. Maybe that's where they were going in the first place."

We were quiet for a while, until Fran spoke: "I just don't get it." Then she thought again. "Well, actually I do. How at her age do you stop yourself, when everything in you is calling you out, and all that holds you back are your parents. And fear. And some vague sense of obligation. To what? Why? And you have to admit, the guy is *really* handsome. I remember when I was seventeen . . ."

"Not now," I said. "Please." Nearing our fifties, which seemed impossible, neither of us looked much like seventeen anymore, though Fran was still slim and attractive, even when she was so tired.

For a time, we were silent again. Through the open window came the wind, and we could hear nuts and twigs blown from the trees.

"She seems so desperate," Fran said in a different tone. "What are we doing wrong?"

"Nothing," I said, trying to be reasonable, but wondering the same thing myself. "They're teenagers."

"But she's *our* teenager." Fran got up, went to the window, looked out, then walked around the room and sat down again, pulling the hem of her robe across her legs. "Sometimes I wonder if we should have stayed here after she was born. Maybe we should have moved somewhere else. Maybe we should move now. For her sake."

I thought, but didn't say, *It wasn't **my** idea to come up here way back when.*

Fran seemed to sense what I was thinking. "Well, I guess this wouldn't be the best time to move, seeing as she's three-quarters through high school." She tried to brush something off the front of her robe. "Should we call the sheriff sometime?"

"There's nothing he can do before morning either. Besides, his boat's in Higgins Bay."

By now it was well after midnight. Six hours later on a normal summer morning, we'd be down in the kitchen, brewing coffee, cooking sausage, and mixing up pancake batter.

Then we heard the annex stairs creak with Nat's slow, light steps. I could recognize them anywhere. At once, I was flooded with relief and anger, the latter the most powerful at the moment. Was she trying to sneak back in, hoping we were asleep in our bedroom?

She appeared in the doorway. Long, stringy, wind-whipped hair. Jeans and rumpled T-shirt. Flip-flops hanging in her hand. Her clothes were dry, so the boat hadn't capsized, but her eyes were red, sunk deep into their hollows, and her eyeliner had tracked down her cheeks. She'd been crying. Something unexpected had happened or not happened, and I could tell it had little to do with the wind and waves, and everything to do with her heart. *Had they fought? On the boat? On the island? On the dock? Was one or both of them drunk? Had Chuck forced himself on her? Was she scared? Or had she thrown herself at him and been rejected, or been used and humiliated? Had they had sex? Her first time? Was it nothing like what she'd imagined?*

Fran leapt up and tried to wrap her arms around her, but Nat pushed her away.

"Can I get you some milk, tea, toast, anything?" I asked foolishly, my anger gone.

Nat didn't say anything.

"Are you all right?" Fran asked.

"Yes. Leave me alone!" Her hands shook. She smelled of nervous sweat, and her voice was a snarl: "I'm going to bed. I don't even know why you're up waiting!"

Fran and I exchanged a glance. "We were worried," I said. "It's a windy night. You were out in the boat. Do you know what time it is?"

Nat didn't answer. I'd never seen her so sad, angry, and hard. She seemed almost proud in her sadness, and she wasn't about to let us into it. "I'm going to bed," she said once more. "And so should you!" She crossed the rug, then, holding her back straight and shoulders square, marched into her room, closed the door, and snapped the lock.

"My baby," Fran said in a wavering voice. "What's going to become of her?"

Hours later, with that vague sense of some absence or presence, I woke and, feeling with my hands and feet, couldn't find Fran sleeping beside me. The wind had died down. I got up, went out of our room, and stood in the dark hall. No one was in the bathroom. There was no light from the living area. Nor was there light beneath Nat's closed door. But there were voices behind it. Familiar ones. I couldn't make out the words, yet I could hear them faintly: Fran's voice, patient, soft, and reassuring. And now and then Nat's, sniffling and hesitant, yet easing a little, smoothing out, like the lake sometimes at twilight.

Of course, I remember that it was rainy and dreary on the weekend after the board meeting near the end of the following October, almost exactly a year ago now. Nat had recently begun her senior year. As fast as Chuck had entered her life, he had disappeared from it, and already the summer seemed like ancient history. Fran and I had grounded Nat for two weekends for going out in the guide-boat and for coming home late that night back in August, and since then we'd imposed some other rules. Now, if Nat went somewhere after school or in the evenings, she had to call when she got there. She either found a ride home by nine, or I picked her up by then, and strictly speaking, she'd abided by these restrictions: she phoned us, she didn't come home late. Nor were there any more harsh words or traumatic scenes. And yet at the same time, she seemed to hold herself even farther away from us. She seldom spoke of her feelings or what she was up to when she wasn't home, and when she did speak of those things, it was only with Fran—and briefly. Together, we all had an uncertain understanding: that as long Nat observed the rules we'd set, one by one we'd relax them.

Anyway, on that dreary late-October weekend, winter was arriving early. Mice had taken up residence in the walls and ceilings, scratching and scurrying around. The Yankees weren't in the World Series. The air smelled of chimney smoke. Wet leaves covered the roads—driven over, they turned into a kind of paste—and in the early mornings when it wasn't raining or sleeting, silvery frost encrusted the knoll, and mist, like a blanket, lay low on the lake.

Because of the bleak weather, the head of a small, bird-watchers group called on that Friday afternoon to cancel their reservations at the last minute. So, unexpectedly, Fran and I had a free evening, which got me thinking and planning.

One thing that happens when you and your spouse are busy innkeepers and living with a hormone-pumped seventeen-year-old: you have to do some clever planning yourselves, that is, if now and then you want to drag your own hormones out of storage. You have to watch for your opportunities, think and act. In the parenting books they don't tell you that occasionally, and for your own good, you should get away from the kids, or in our circumstances, the kid.

So, after I'd put down the phone that afternoon, and as Nat and Fran were upstairs and out of earshot, I picked it up again. I called Vera at the Cedar View and made sure she was serving dinner that evening. Then I called Clyde Phelps who owns and manages the Sea Horse Motel down near Wells. I asked him if he had any rooms available.

He laughed. "Oh, I think I can squeeze someone in. What's up? You're not overflowing *this* weekend?"

I said no, today was Fran's and my anniversary—a lie, but not a terribly big one, as it was just a month or so off. I said we wanted to "get away for a few hours this evening," and Clyde understood immediately.

"Take room five," he said. "The best I've got. Hey, I'll even turn on the heat! It's on me. I'll leave the key in the door."

Upstairs, I told Fran that the bird-watchers had just cancelled and, if she wanted, we could make it over to Orma's for one of those Friday night potluck dinners.

She said great, she'd make a casserole to take, but first we should check to make sure our plans were okay with Nat. Since the end of that summer, Fran and I had gone out a few of times on our own when we had no guests, leaving Nat alone at the inn for the evening. Twice we went to the movies with the Wagoners, and once for pizza with Flora Abrams. While Fran and I were away, Nat was allowed to talk on the phone, but she had to stay home, and she couldn't have any visitors. Those were among the rules that we'd set down and she'd apparently followed so far.

As I've mentioned, cell phones are useless around here, so each time before Fran and I left on those evenings, we'd give Nat the number where we could be reached. From wherever we'd gone to, we'd call her after an hour or so, and either she would be on the phone, or, most likely, she'd be watching TV. By eleven, Fran and I would return home, another rule, though unspoken. As we'd come down the driveway, we'd see through the trees that flickering pale light in the annex window, which meant that we'd find Nat sound asleep on the sofa, curled under a blanket, the TV droning on.

When we checked with her on that October late-afternoon, Nat said in her usual monotone, "Go ahead to the potluck. Have a good time." She said she was wrung out after a rotten, eighth period trigonometry test, so tonight she'd probably just watch the tube and go to bed.

"You feeling all right?" Fran asked her. "You look a little washed out. Maybe you're coming down with a fever. We can go some other time."

"I'm fine," Nat said. "Fine" was a word that covered her every conceivable emotion and condition. Everything was always "fine."

"You sure?" Fran asked.

"Yes. Scram!"

Normally, Nat would get her own dinner on evenings when Fran and I went out, but on that one, Fran insisted on making a sandwich that she left downstairs on the kitchen table, with chips, cookies, and an apple. Again she asked Nat if she'd rather we stayed home.

"How many times do I have to tell you? I'm fine. Just go."

So Fran and I left the inn at six-thirty in the same prehistoric van that we drove when we'd first come up here. We had a curried chicken and rice casserole on the console between us, the top of the big porcelain pot held on with a thick rubber band. When we got onto Route 8 but didn't turn into Orma's, Fran looked at me, surprised, and said, "Hey, you missed it! What's going on?"

"I'm abducting you."

She laughed. "Where are you abducting me *to*?"

"It's a surprise."

The side of her face squinched up a little. "But how will Nat know where we are?"

"We'll call as soon as we get there," I said. "It's not far."

From Orma's, it takes about twenty more minutes to get to the Cedar View along that two-lane stretch of road that follows the Kunjamuck River for a while, then winds gracefully through the low mountains. Had it been a clear evening, it would have been a spectacular ride, the maples on fire with the setting sun, the last of the aspen leaves winking like coins, and the stark white trunks of the birches standing out against the pines.

As it was, things were misty and shrouded. A gray ceiling cut off all the peaks. Now and then I turned on the spastic wipers. At the moment, it wasn't raining, but drops splattered down from overhanging trees. We lugged up hills, and coming down them, I mashed the brakes, and we held on around the curves.

As we rode, Fran and I didn't talk a lot, but I could tell by the way that she kept her mouth small that she was quietly intrigued. She always liked surprises—good ones, that is—and she always liked surprising others.

When we sputtered into the Cedar View, Fran couldn't hide her pleasure. "Dinner?"

"I thought we'd nix off the curried chicken and rice."

"Wonderful!" She bent over the casserole and kissed me. "I'm glad I put on a skirt."

The Cedar View is the only restaurant for miles where you can order fish that isn't fried, where bread is baked on the premises, and on each of the tables a candle stands beside an arrangement of fresh wild flowers or sprigs of fern or balsam—a big step up from the Tumble Inn.

At the reception desk, while Fran was in the ladies' room, I phoned Nat, told her of our switch in plans, that Fran and I were having a special dinner out together, and I gave her the number at the Cedar View.

As if she'd rather not be interrupted, she said, "I'm *trying* to do some homework."

I hung up, and when Fran came back, she asked, "She okay?"

"She says she's doing her homework."

"Really? That's a nice surprise," Fran said, taking my arm.

Vera led us to the table looking out the picture widow toward the ravine that disappeared with the dusk. Over dinner, we talked about the things you talk about at that time of year if you're Adirondack innkeepers. Laying up wood. Airing out the quilts. And of course, we also talked about Nat. How she'd actually done okay on the preliminary standardized aptitude tests, but she wasn't much interested in things academic. Knock wood, though, she'd squeak through. The schools up here graduate almost everyone to keep expenses and taxes low. So less than a year from then, we figured, Nat should be out of high school, possibly working and off on her own. Like most of her classmates, she didn't seem college-bound.

That bothered both of us, but Fran a little less so. "She'll be okay," Fran said with a kind of brave hopefulness that might have had something to do with the candlelight and the glass of Chablis she'd ordered. "Give her some time. Eventually, she'll pull herself together. She'll find her place in the world."

Then what would *we* do? Keep going as innkeepers? Much more often than me, Fran thought about these things. Life, for her, was a series of interesting options, a map with roads that kept forking. You always have choices, she said. You can always change course. That, after all, is how we'd gotten up here. If and when the time was right, we could move, do something else.

"Like what?" I asked across our small table.

She rattled off a number of possibilities, only the last of which I remember. Maybe we could eventually run a bed and breakfast somewhere, something less strenuous than keeping an old inn on a huge piece of property in the Adirondacks. Maybe a bungalow on the Jersey shore, where there weren't these long, cold winters, and we could be closer to our parents.

We went on in this whimsical, speculative way, which was pleasant with Vera's lemon trout and baked potatoes, and when the changes we'd been thinking about didn't seem very pressing. In the candlelight, Fran's eyes seemed both intense and relaxed. At their corners, like at the corners of mine, skin wrinkled when she smiled. She was wearing a silver necklace, thin as a filament, and her maroon cable-knit sweater that still nipped in at her waist. Her hair wasn't really red anymore, but dusky auburn, a few shades darker than Nat's, and with some threads of gray mixed in. Now she kept it at shoulder length, neat but never prissy. It flared when she turned her head.

When it was time for dessert, I said, "Let's wait," and drawing out what suspense I could: "Before we go home, before we call it an evening, we have one more stop."

"You're kidding. Where?" she asked.

"It's another surprise."

"How long will we be there?"

"That depends."

"On what?"

"Well, I guess that depends on us."

Again Fran gave me her quizzical, bemused look, though this time, perhaps just feeling the drift of things, she didn't ask how Nat would know where we'd be. I paid the check, said thanks to Vera, and we went out and got in the van.

The Sea Horse is just a few more miles down the road, past the boarded-up Mountaineer ice cream shop and the cutoff to Gilmantown. Even in the pitch black, you can't miss it. Along a rare straightaway north of Wells, the blue neon flickers in Clyde's office window:

SEA HORSE MO EL
Heated
Vacancy

I turned in. My headlights swept the ten identical units lined up and attached to the office, each with a window and a door with a stenciled number on it and a plastic chair on a slab of concrete beneath a tiny porch roof. All the units were dark, save for one in the middle, where a slot of light squeezed through the draperies. I pulled up to it, my front bumper nudging the standing, half-buried tires that marked the end of the gravel lot and the beginning of so many dreams.

Here and there in the lower Adirondacks, you can still find these old motels that, if you are of a particular age or disposition, will draw you in off the roads. Built in the late fifties, during the first flush of motorized, middle-class honeymooning and vacationing, a place like this was what you were shooting for after a long and winding journey. Though the bedsprings were mushy, you could count on clean sheets and towels, vacuumed floors, and a couple of miniature bars of soap stacked beside the bathroom sink.

We got out of the car and walked through the drizzling rain and onto the porch, guided by the slot of light. The key, as Clyde had said, was in the door. I opened it and followed Fran inside.

You've probably heard of the "Adirondack style." More or less, it's been copied at the Tumble Inn: pine twig furniture, balsam pillows, crossed snowshoes or skis above the granite hearth, birch bark picture frames, door handles made of antlers. All the great, wild north woods tamed and hauled indoors.

There is also, however, a less celebrated *anti*-Adirondack style, practiced mainly by certain headstrong Year-Rounders who live outside the villages: lime-green clapboard with orange shutters, pink flamingoes in front yards, and along the driveways those bright, whirling pinwheel things that resemble sunflowers. To hell with the woods, the cold, and the tang of balsam, they seem to say. To hell with everything up here. Give us heat, color, and blaring sun, and if the weather and geography won't comply, then by God, we'll do it ourselves!

Room #5 of the Sea Horse was a variant of this aesthetic. Everything in it was oceanic or, more particularly, Caribbean. Shells and chunks of coral clung to turquoise walls. A piece of driftwood, smooth as whale bone, lay on the linoleum in a corner. Beside a phone, and an ashtray in the shape of a halved coconut, stood a lamp fashioned from some sort of buoy, and a fine-meshed fishing net, a seine, covered the bed. As Clyde had turned the baseboard heaters on high, this cinder block room in the chill Adirondacks almost felt downright sultry. If you'd closed your eyes in determined imagination, you might even have seen palms on white beaches, and heard the surf and plinking steel drums.

By now, after I'd closed the door behind us, we were looking around, and I couldn't read the message in Fran's shoulders, which seemed at once to rise and droop. We were not yet old, but neither were we young. We certainly weren't the same people who, eighteen years before, had raced up the brook. Perhaps when we actually got down to it, this sort of thing—stealing away like a couple of teenagers, while our own teenager should be waiting at home—perhaps this didn't behoove us. And perhaps it wouldn't even have its desired effect, seeing as our bodies and vital equipment, no great shakes to begin with, were getting more cranky, slower to warm, and, like the van, a little iffy on the hills. Was the heat that poured from the baseboards sultry? Or was it cloying and stifling? I doubted that lamps made from buoys were Fran's cup of tea. Nor the briny smell of old fishing nets.

We took it all in. A low-rent tryst with your spouse. By that time of our lives, we'd become more cautious with one another, as you are in certain shops that sell pottery and glass. I don't think this meant that we wanted each other less. In fact, it was quite the opposite. The merchandise on the shelves just seemed more delicate and fragile, and our hands less sure of themselves. In a strange way, this made us feel older *and* younger: older because our flesh was changing, we were more self-conscious, our reactions less certain—and younger for just the same reasons.

"So this is the place we've been getting to?" Fran asked dubiously, still checking out the decor.

"The best I could do under the circumstances," I said. "There aren't a lot of options."

To the left of a closet was a small bathroom with aquamarine tile. Fran went in, closing the door behind her, and soon I heard the faucet turned on, off, then running again for what seemed a long time.

I took off my coat and scarf, sat down on the edge of the bed, and of course the mattress bowed and the springs twanged. I heard a car approach on the road and fly past, the *shish*-ing sound of tires on wet pavement, heading downhill and south. Then the sound of the car faded. Its taillights, I imagined, brightened as they receded, the car braking around the bend. Then the road would be dark and quiet again, as if the car had never happened. I looked at my watch. It was 10:30, and we were a half hour from home.

When Fran came out, she didn't look very different, except that she'd left her coat on the hook on the bathroom door, and she seemed at once more relaxed and resolved. She'd taken off her necklace. She'd pushed up her sleeves and pulled her hair behind her ears, as if getting down to business. As she came to the bed, she was looking at me openly, full in the face, in that way that still makes me think and feel: *This is my wife. Fran.* This place wasn't the greatest, her eyes were saying, but somehow we'd gotten here—*Here we are!*—and together we'd make the best of it. We might even make a pretty good thing of it, something we'd both remember.

I called the inn before we'd dressed, even before we'd untangled ourselves from the fishing net, but there was no answer. Or rather, after five rings, I heard my own slow, courteous recorded voice: "Thank you for calling The Tumble Inn, a historic four season inn overlooking beautiful White Birch

Lake in the Adirondack Mountains. We can't come to the phone right now, so please leave your name, number, and a brief message, and we'll get back to you as soon as possible."

I hung up and called again.

Again the recorded message.

My stomach lurched. That sudden queasiness. *Where has she gone? What has she done?* "She's not picking up," I said.

"That's odd. Let me try," Fran said, sitting up. "You might have mis-dialed."

"But that was *our* recording!" My voice was louder than I'd intended. "That was *our* number!"

No matter. She squiggled off the bed, the net all twisted around her thighs. She pushed the buttons on the phone. She waited, counting the rings. Now both of us were standing up. It was 11:45.

"The damn recording!" Fran said, holding the receiver like something she couldn't recognize. Then, her eyes wide, she put it down. "I don't understand. Why isn't she answering? If she's there, she barely has to reach to get the phone."

Fran wriggled out of the net and threw it aside. With her free hand, she pulled a blanket up to her chest and clamped it there with one arm. Her eyes dug into me. "I had a strange feeling when we left. Where is she, Mark? Is she sick? Has she gone somewhere? What in the world has happened?"

"How am I supposed to know?" I said, though I had some suspicion involving boys, beer, and cars.

For a moment, we were quiet. Then, brightening, Fran said, "Hold on. Wait a second. Maybe she's just in the bathroom. Of course. As soon as she's out, she'll answer!" She took stock of the room again, almost laughing, putting her hand over her mouth. "Goodness, what a mess. Just look at us!"

We waited a few minutes and then a few extra minutes. Another car flew by, heading south.

Then Fran pushed the phone buttons once more. She groaned as the recording came on, and this time she left a message. "Sweetie. Honey pie. *Baby*!" Names we hadn't called Nat in years, names that boys might already be calling her. "Sweetie, can you hear me? We're on our way. We'll be right home. Love you."

She slammed down the receiver.

I wish I could have been more calm, but I said, "Let's get out of here!" and Fran was of a similar mind.

We scrambled for clothes amid the driftwood and coral. How, in a small room, could things be so dispersed? *Where are my underpants? To hell with my underpants. Where is Fran's bra? To hell with that, too!* Pants, belt, blouse, skirt, sweater, no tights, mis-buttoned shirt, tails hanging out, shoes, laces untied. In the rush, I knocked over the buoy-shaped lamp, shattering the bulb. We left it. We left everything. We didn't even leave a note apologizing for the lamp. *We never set foot in this place!*

We grabbed our coats.

Then the door.

Then the van, the road, and the night.

More than the smell of old fishing nets, more than any other smell, it's curry that really gets to me. Just a year ago, a young couple from India somehow found their way around the globe to Indian Lake, about forty-five minutes north of here, and they opened what I believe is the first authentic Indian restaurant in the Adirondacks. It's still in business, evidently it's pretty good, and you can go there today if you want to. But I'm afraid I'll have to bow out. I don't like being surprised by certain memories in public places, and often it's the smell of things that hurtles me back.

That night, as you know, was raw, the road slick, and the van was iffy on the hills, most of which on the trip north from the Sea Horse are of the steep variety. So for the most part, the going was painfully slow, no matter how hard I pushed the gas pedal. Like a trucker, I put on speed coming down the hills, and going up, I held our momentum as long as I could, until we'd slow down, both of us rocking back and forth in our seats, as if to push us over the tops. We didn't say much, just stared ahead to the farthest reach of the headlights. On that stretch of road, there are hardly any houses, so along the sides, we just felt the forest, the big, thick darkness of it, and only now and then we'd see a tiny, pitiful red reflector that someone had stuck to a tree. We passed the Gilmantown cutoff, a hole in the dark that veered to the left, but this was no time for a scenic drive over the mountains. We passed the Cedar View, or the place that I knew was the Cedar View, by then all black, closed up for the night, Vera having blown out the candles, finished the dishes, tossed the garbage out back in the Dumpster, then hit the lights.

We were still seven or eight miles away from the inn at that point, when I started making bargains with whatever God might be watching us, and I had the feeling that Fran, all folded into her coat, was thinking along the same lines: *We won't sneak off anymore. We won't be deceptive. We won't ever do anything like this again. . . . If only Nat's asleep on the sofa or in bed, or down in the kitchen having a snack. Or even if she's mad at us for being so late. Or even if she's off with some guy in an old Camaro parked in the weeds beside the dirt road. . . . Even that would be okay. We'd settle for that. Anything that isn't irreparable.*

Then came those little tricks of optimism. I let them wash over me. *The phone in the annex was stone dead,* the cord by some accident pulled out of the wall, while the phone still working down in the office rang and rang until the recording came on. So of course Nat wouldn't have heard our phone calls, never mind running downstairs in time to pick up the receiver. Or: *She was in the shower,* one of her marathon monsoon showers, the door closed, her CD player booming, she singing at the top of her lungs, and the water smashing down. No way she could hear *anything* over that! Only by now, as we passed the Mountaineer on our way home, would she finally be stepping out through the bathroom door in a billow of steam, stepping in that tiptoed way of hers, wrapping herself in a towel from chest to knees, another like a turban around her hair, and that smell of her shampoo, sweet as apricots.

We turned onto Route 8, the high beams on. Not a car on the road, not a house alongside. The road unwound like an over-stretched spring. Rags of mist hung in valleys. As we lugged up the hill before Alder Pond, the wipers flailed out of sync.

"Can't we go any faster?" Fran said.

We came over the crest and were gaining speed, when I saw the mist faintly glowing at the bottom of the hill where the road curved left through a tunnel of sugar maples. The glow brightened. I touched the brakes and clicked my headlights down. The glow brightened, then resolved into two parallel columns that lit up the beautiful red and orange undersides of the remaining leaves. *Doesn't he see we're coming? Can't he switch off his high beams?*

I flashed my headlights, but the columns swung like spotlights in our direction. We entered the turn, and the lights themselves shown directly upon us. They were flying at us, bigger and bigger. *Doesn't he see us? Is he blind?*

I flashed my headlights again. I pounded the brakes. I spun the wheel to the left. Tires screamed and slid on wet leaves. He was still coming, those lights the only things left in the world. *Good God, doesn't he see . . . ?*

And then Fran made a surprised little sound, like "Oh!"

And then. . . . Well, that's all I remember. . . .

Until I was sitting beside a guardrail, cold and shaking, with a poncho around my back and shoulders. Everywhere lights swirled, glass glittered, radios squawked, and there was the strangest, spicy smell. Even before I recognized it, I knew that it didn't belong here, not here in the Adirondack woods in the rain. It took me a while to figure out. It was curry. Yes. On my arms, on my shirt, on my pants, in my hair and ears, everywhere—those little clinging grains of rice, almost like after a wedding.

It was Jim Owen, our sheriff, who told me. He's an easy-going guy from Higgins Bay, though I can't say I know him real well. We wave when we pass on the roads, and we talk baseball at the market or at Stephenson's.

He came over after the ambulance guys had checked me out and helped me get back on my feet.

"How long was I out of it?" was the first thing I said.

"I'm not sure," he said in his low voice. He wore a yellow raincoat. His face looked drained, his eyes gray. "You were coming to when we got here and pulled you out of the van. If you're still feeling woozy, we can take you to the hospital for observation."

"No," I said, though I still must have been pretty dazed and numb. My left arm was sore, but I could move it. "I think I'm okay."

He shook his head. "Amazing."

"Where's Fran?" I asked.

He took my elbow and said, "Let's get out of this weather. Come, get in my car."

We walked around the glass, twisted metal, and scraps of plastic on the road. The red and blue lights whirled on top of his cruiser, making everything flash. He opened the door and guided me inside where it was warm and dry, the engine idling. Then he went back around the car, got in behind the wheel, and turned off the radio. He's a heavyset, round-shouldered guy who puts his seat way back. His fingers are blunt, like a plumber's fingers, his voice as soft as a librarian's. He took off his wet, visored hat that had something like a shower cap covering it. He ran his big hands through his thinning hair. Then on his lap, he turned them palms up and opened them wide. He looked right at me. "Mark, she took the full force of the crash. It crushed in the passenger door. It must have killed her instantly. I'm sorry."

I remember my eyes blinking, and I remember all that flashing outside. Somehow it was like watching a movie, and yet the movie seemed the same as what was actually happening. There were Jim and me in his cruiser. There was his hat. There was the poncho around my shoulders. There were his big hands. There were my own hands, limp and powerless, like something fallen into my lap. But how, at the same time, was I watching this movie and *in* it? Was I really there? Were these my hands? Was this really happening to me?

After a while, Jim asked, "What in the world is that smell? And the rice?"

"Curry. Fran made it." My voice was strange and flat. It sounded like someone else's voice from inside my throat, and yet from far away.

"You want a tissue or something? It's all over you."

"I have to get home," I said.

"I'm afraid we have paperwork to do, even at a time like this." He took the metal clipboard from a big magnet on the front dash. "I've got to ask you some questions. Then we have to go down to Johnstown. To make the ID."

"But Nat," I said. "She's at home. I think. Or at least that's where we left her. And I'm late."

He let out a breath and put his clipboard back on the dash. He's a father. He has a daughter, Silvie, a sixth-grader, of his own. "Okay, I'll take you home," he said.

After he'd gotten out and spoken to another man in a raincoat, he got back in the car. He turned off his whirling lights, and the man lifted a ribbon of yellow tape so we could drive under it.

In a way, it was just a continuation of my trip home from the Sea Horse. The headlights bored into the darkness, a couple of reflectors whipped past, and now and then a guardrail popped up, ran alongside us for a while, then dipped and disappeared. In another way, the sheriff and I were like a couple of old bucks heading home to waiting wives after staying too late at the Oxbow, not sure if we should slow down to put off what was coming to us, or to speed up to get it over with. In yet another way, the trip was like nothing I'd ever known. The wipers actually moved in unison. The heater worked. The brakes didn't throb. The engine purred. We climbed right up the hills. And I was in the passenger seat. How odd.

Jim and I didn't talk a lot.

"You sure you're all right?" he asked, glancing at me.

Again, I said I was.

At another point he said, "That guy in the other car. From over in Bakers Mills. He smelled like a brewery. He was blind drunk. He didn't make it either."

Then a while later, he said, "It's going to be a long one," by which he might have been referring to that particular night, or to the entire winter. In any case, he was probably right, so I nodded yes.

Along his dashboard, gauges glowed and winked. A digital clock said 2:05.

We passed Orma's. No lights upstairs, just that gray tinge through her store windows from the Coke machine in back. The potluck dinner must have been long over, the card tables folded up and put away, the casserole dishes taken home and washed, everyone asleep.

We turned onto the dirt road. We rumbled over stones and splashed through potholes. We went through the marsh, over the plank bridge, and around the hairpin turn. The trees pressed in. The road narrowed. We thumped into the driveway, the headlights careening across the knoll, illuminating the bushes I'd planted and the swing set I'd reinforced and repainted, I don't know how many times over the years.

We parked in the lot, and Jim shut off the engine. The lake was gone in the dark and drizzle, but you could feel it out there, deep, long, and wide.

"You want me to come in?" he asked. "I can hang around for a while, if you and Nat want some company. I could make you some tea or something."

"No thanks," I said. He was very kind, maybe as kind as a person could be. I told him to get himself home. Sally, his wife, must be wondering. It was awfully late.

He said, "All right. I'll pick you up in the morning. Eight o'clock. We'll deal with the paperwork and the rest. In the meantime, I'm going to call the Wagoners and let them know."

We were still speaking with a strange calm. There was still that flatness in my voice. I said I'd be ready at eight and thanked him again. I knew that bringing me right home from a fatal accident was against all accepted procedure. He hadn't even gotten a statement from me, to say nothing of writing a report. He was bound to catch hell for this, even up here where procedures can get pretty loose. But like I said, he was a father.

"Go on in and see your daughter," he said. "Take care. Call me if you want to talk. See you in the morning."

I got out of his cruiser and began walking across the knoll. The air was cold and still. The drizzle had turned to frost on the grass. A few leaves crunched beneath my shoes. Coming around the hemlocks, I saw the lantern shining beside the porch door, but the rest of the inn was dark. Just a thick shape that came out of the woods. The roof was a line against the charcoal sky, interrupted by the triangular dormers. The chimney poked up. The TV antenna stood with its splayed fingers. The windows were black as coal.

That's when I really started to feel it, I think. The little tingles in my fingers and at the back of my neck. This wasn't a movie about someone else. *Is anybody home?* For a moment, I couldn't breathe.

When I moved again, I climbed the stairs to the porch. I heard Jim start his engine and pull out of the driveway. In that slow, intermittent way that it happens up here, the sound faded into the forest.

I went inside and switched on the hall light. Everything seemed so untouched, unchanged, so ordinary. The clock ticked on the wall above the reception desk. The guest book lay open to the same page. There was the ballpoint pen on its little beaded chain. There was the service bell and the pink While You Were Out pad. Nothing was scribbled on it.

In the dining room, the tables were still set for the bird-watchers group that had cancelled their reservations. Chrysanthemums were on the side table. When I turned on the fluorescent light, the kitchen jumped alive, but I didn't pause to look around. I went up the back stairs to the annex, my hand on the wobbly railing. The steps creaked. I felt for the knob, opened the door into our living area, and switched on the lamp.

Nat wasn't asleep on the sofa. Nor was her pillow there. Nor were her things on the table or floor. The TV was off. The phone sat quietly. The blanket lay on the edge of the sofa, neat as a folded flag.

Down the short hallway, the door to Fran's and my bedroom stood open, but I didn't go in there. I couldn't. Instead, I went straight to Nat's door which was open part way. Slowly, I pushed it until I could slip through. I say "slip" because I felt stealthy. I was always supposed to knock on her door. That's the rule with a teenage daughter, even if you don't think she's inside.

In her room, it was too dark to see. I knew where everything was supposed to be, which was never where it was. So I moved carefully with my arms outstretched and my feet feeling the space in front of me. It's a tiny room that was always crammed with Nat's things, the floor a minefield of sneakers, shoes, strewn clothes, teen magazines, her laptop, and often a lamp on an extension cord. When she studied—if she studied—she sprawled on the rug. That way blood would go to her brain, she always told me, "where I do my thinking." Her desk, of course, was reserved for items more important than books: cosmetics, radio, CD player, bracelets, little cedar boxes filled with who-knows-what, plastic do-dads from vending machines—all those things that she calls her own and that tell her who she is.

I stumbled into her backpack. I stepped on a pencil and a spiral notebook. Bending low, I touched the side of her bureau, and then the cool metal frame of her bed. Then the box spring. The sheeted mattress. Then on her pillow: the long, smooth strands of her hair. Where they'd clung together, they were damp. And that smell: apricot!

So she *had* been in the shower while we were calling from the Sea Horse! She'd been here all along!

I heard her turn in her sleep, but she didn't wake up. And listening carefully, I could hear her breath, soft, slow, and even. Sometime after our string of phone calls, she must have come out of the bathroom, turned off the TV, folded the blanket, taken her pillow, and on her way in here, switched off the lamp.

She kept on breathing. And I wanted to be *inside* that breathing, *inside* her dreams, whatever they were. And a long way from waking up.

So I didn't wake her. I let her be. I went out her door, to the bathroom, where I got out of the poncho and my curried clothes, and got into my pajamas. Then I took the blanket from the sofa and went back into Nat's room. In the dark, I cleared a space on the rug and lay down with the things of her life, pulling the blanket over me. I listened to the night sounds of the inn, the creaks, groans, and tapping radiator pipes, and once I thought I heard a car in the driveway, but I wasn't sure. Mostly I listened to Nat's breathing. In and out. An amazing thing. That was all that mattered.

For the rest of that night, I didn't sleep. I just lay there listening, until the bluish dawn seeped through her curtains, and I saw Nat's long shape under her blankets, with her head on her hands, turned toward me.

Then she opened her eyes.

How can a child absorb the worst news imaginable? How can anyone? How could I?

"Mom and I were in a car crash," I said, weeping. I was sitting now on the edge of Nat's bed. I put my hand on the blanket where it covered her arm. Then, unbelievably, I said, "Honey, I'm sorry. She didn't make it. She isn't here anymore."

Nat didn't say anything, but I could feel her arm tense. While I tried to describe what I remembered of the accident, she moved and sat up beside me with her legs together, her heels on the bed frame and her knees to her chest, making a tent of her nightgown. Her face was pale. She stared at the rug. She didn't cry, but started to tremble. Her arms hugged her shins, as if to squeeze herself into the smallest shape and to keep from shaking apart.

Trembling myself, I told her I loved her. I told her, "I'll never leave you. I promise." I must have said that half a dozen times. I meant it with every fiber of my being, and she nodded slowly, which I think was her way of saying that she'd heard me.

"Where is she?" Nat asked.

"In Johnstown," I said, as if Fran was out shopping. I told Nat that the sheriff would be here in a couple of hours. He was supposed to drive me down there, "but I'm not about to go anywhere without you." "I'll never leave you," I said again and again.

Then, without saying anything else, she got off the bed and slid into her pink, furry slippers, which still made her look like a kid. I followed her out her door, through our living area, and down the stairs, where I smelled coffee brewing. In the kitchen, the lamp was lit on the table, and in its yellow glow sat Bruce and Lena Wagoner in rumpled shirts and jeans, and with their hair sticking out. Evidently, they'd heard from Jim, thrown on whatever clothes were at hand, and had driven right over. In the wee hours, they must have quietly let themselves in, and ever since had been sitting here, waiting to see us, hands touching across the table. Their faces were pale and their eyes were red. Their shoelaces, I remember, were untied. Together they stood, took us into their big arms, and I could feel their bodies shuddering.

"Coffee. We made coffee," was all Lena could say, tears rolling down her cheeks.

"And cornbread," Bruce said. "Sit. Eat. It's good to eat. Please."

They poured coffee and orange juice and cut squares of cornbread. We sat, and the coffee and cornbread were good, but we could only sip and eat a little.

"Thanks," I said, and I really meant that, but I may not have fully conveyed it.

Then Nat got up, went through the swinging doors, through the dining room, and into the living room, as I followed and the Wagoners stayed in the kitchen, giving us space while letting us know they'd be there. Nat opened the curtains. Outside, the morning had come, the drizzle had stopped, the grass was still frosted, and everywhere the air had cleared, except for that blanket of mist, about four feet high that covered the lake, thick as beaten egg whites. In summers, the hot air warms the upper layer of lake water, which floats on deeper, cooler water. But by mid-October, the cold night air chills that upper layer. It becomes more dense than the water below, which causes it to sink, while the lower, now warmer layers rise to the top. In this way, the lake literally "turns over." That's how we describe it. What's shallow sinks. What's deep rises to the surface. And while you can't really see this, you can tell it's happening by that thick, low mist on the lake, the condensation of evaporating water, on crisp fall mornings.

"How did it happen?" Nat asked, not looking at me, but straight out the picture window toward the lake. Her hair was long and tangled.

I'd already told her, but I told her again: about the turn near Alder Pond, the headlights, the sound of the tires. I didn't tell her the time of the accident, nor that we were returning from the Sea Horse.

"Did she say anything at the end?"

"She just said, 'Oh,' like she was surprised. I don't remember anything else. It happened so fast."

In a moment, she said, "I wish I could have told her something."

"What?"

"Something." Then she was quiet.

And although I couldn't take it all in just then, I was suddenly a man without a wife, a single father, and she a teenage girl without her mother. In a second, our lives had changed absolutely, and while our pain would mingle in many places, in others it would never touch.

"What's going to happen to me?" Nat asked in a voice I could barely hear.

"You'll be okay," I said. "We'll stay together. You and me. We'll try to be okay. All right?"

Again she gave that slow, absent nod, and after another moment she said in a tone that meant I shouldn't follow, "I'm going down to the water."

She went into the hall and put on her jacket. It was one of those navy-blue pea jackets that lots of kids were wearing that year. The collar up. Shoulders hunched as in a bitter wind. Hands shoved into pockets. It could make you look hard, an outcast, like James Dean. But she was still wearing her nightgown that showed below it, and those pink, furry slippers.

"I'll be right here," I said as she moved toward the door. Yet again, I said, "I'll never leave you."

Through the window I watched her in that ridiculous outfit as she went across the knoll, stepping gingerly as you do though shallow puddles, leaving her prints in the frost. She followed the path through the glistening field downhill to the beach and the boathouse. She turned onto the dock which disappeared into the mist where it reached beyond the shore. Walking slowly out there, Nat also disappeared, in part. The mist came up above her waist, and with her legs invisible, the rest of her seemed to slide like a chess piece, until she stopped near the end of the dock. There she stood looking out where the hills and island floated on the mist, and where you couldn't see any water.

What was she doing? I don't know. She seemed to be waiting. For what?

If she was waiting for the mist to rise, it didn't happen. If she was waiting for it to burn off in the sun, it didn't happen. Nor did it break up and drift away on a breeze. It just stayed there, unrelenting.

For ten or fifteen minutes, she stood as I watched her, and I think I saw in her what I feared for myself. She looked so small and alone.

Then I couldn't help it. I put on my coat, went out the door, and ran across the knoll, down the hill, across the beach, and onto the dock. The planks, as usual, were warped and sagged under my steps. The whole structure tilted slightly. Each winter the ice heaves and twists it. Slowing down, I came up and stood behind Nat, both of us looking out over the mist. All I wanted was to take her into my arms, to hold her and keep holding her with all my might. Yet somehow it seemed—to both of us, I think—that to touch just then could shatter everything, everything being so brittle.

Still, I put my hand on her arm, and she let it stay, until we turned and walked back down the dock and into what remained of our lives.

14

Then came that terrible time, heavy as iron, some of which is a dark blur to me now, though certain moments stand out in their darkness.

Without Fran, Nat and I didn't know how to *be* with one another. Though literally familiar, we seemed almost like strangers. It was hard to speak. It was hard to even look at each other. I couldn't read Nat's moods, except that they were all inconsolably sad, and I doubt that she could read mine any better. There was a deadness in her eyes, and awkwardly I hugged her, thinking I might wring that deadness out. But I couldn't. She just went limp in my arms. I felt a desperate need to keep her in sight or within my hearing, as if when she went through a doorway or around a corner, I might never see her again. In the evenings, I listened in the hallway as she wept in the shower. When I heard her get up in the middle of the night, I'd sit up in bed, wound like a spring. *Where is she going?* I'd count her footsteps as she'd walk to the bathroom then return to her room, and I'd hear her door click as she shut it.

Yet at other times, in my own sadness, I drifted away and lost track of Nat. I could be anywhere, doing anything, like standing upstairs, looking out the bedroom window toward the woods, and all at once I'd see those high beams turning like spotlights through the mist, getting bigger and bigger. Again I'd hear Fran in the passenger seat saying, "Oh!" And then I heard her saying, "Oh! Oh!" in a weirdly similar way, and I felt her moving beneath or above me. Both of us moving. The heat and sweat. Her taut, freckled muscles and tendons. And always her bones, those long, sharp, insistent bones. . . .

And sometimes that "Oh!" was a cry of intolerable pain, and I thought of her writhing, like waves were pounding through her. We were under the kitchen table. That smell of the sea. Her back arching and collapsing. Her face a fist. . . . And now this strange, slick, bloody thing wriggling like a fish in my hands. . . .

Then the next thing you know, I'd be imagining the drunk behind the wheel of the other car, the idiot who didn't slow down, who kept coming right at us, who made all this happen. I hated his guts. The sonofabitch. At times, I even took some terrible satisfaction in his death—it served him right!—and I thought that somehow it might balance Fran's, though of course it didn't. It just made everything worse. As I heard through the grapevine and later read in the *Hamilton County News,* his name was Pete Rudway, a member of the Elks, a volunteer fireman, a fork lift operator at the sawmill in Weavertown, and he'd had a wife, now a widow, and two young kids, now without a father.

And there were moments, too, when inexplicably I got angry at Fran, when I couldn't believe she'd do this to me, dragging me up here all those years ago, and now leaving me like this, alone with Nat, a teenager for Christ's sake. *Now* what would Fran think about our moving here? Was it worth it?

Then I'd wonder what the accident was like for her. *A stab of fear. A blaze of blackness. Nothing.*

Then I'd turn on myself. I, of course, had been behind the wheel. Fran's death wasn't her doing. It was my idea to go to the Sea Horse and head back late, when everyone knows that the drivers at that hour are guys going somewhere from bars. What the hell did I think I was doing? If only we'd stayed home with Nat. If only I wasn't thinking with my loins. Didn't Fran have a strange feeling about our leaving? What if we'd just gone to the potluck dinner, as I said we would? Or what if I'd called it a night after we'd finished eating at the Cedar View? It was still early then, fewer drunks on the road. Surely we'd have made it home safely. . . .

Then sometimes I wondered why, in that instant before the crash, I'd jerked the wheel to the *left*. Was it just chance? Or an impulse? An instinct? To save myself? But in so doing, I'd turned Fran's door toward the onrushing car. Why didn't I have the instinct, the courage, or whatever to steer to the right? What would have happened then? Would I have died and Fran lived? Would that have been better? Better for Nat? My God, how could I even think these things?

After Nat and I had turned in the mist and walked back down the dock on that morning after the accident, we went up to the inn, where the Wagoners had already been through the refrigerator and were chopping vegetables and cooking stew in the kitchen. In the annex, I called Fran's parents. It was six-thirty. I woke them, and Fran's mother must have thought she was in a nightmare. When I'd told her what had happened, she kept asking who I was and how was she supposed to believe it was me. She said I didn't sound like myself. Nor did she sound like *her*self: "Are you sure? Are you sure?" she asked, her voice cracking. "You're talking about Fran? *My* Fran? That's ridiculous! *My* daughter? Dead?" And then after I'd answered yes again and again, she cried, "No! No!" Then stony silence. And then the line clicking dead.

I called my own parents, and I remember my mother's tone, her calm and eerie practicality when she was stunned or staggered. "Where are you now? Are you safe? Is Nat with you? Is anyone else with you? Have you eaten? Are you warm? Stay where you are. We'll be there as soon as we can."

As Jim Owen had promised, he arrived at exactly eight that morning and drove Nat and me to Johnstown in his cruiser. While Nat waited outside in the funeral home lobby, a solemn man in a dark coat and tie took me into a small room smelling of antiseptic where, beneath a hanging florescent light, a body lay on a gurney. It was Fran. There on her forearms were her pale freckles. There were her wrists with those bird-like bones fanning across the backs of her hands. There were her long, tapered thumbs, almost as long as her other fingers. There was the hollow in that V of bones at the base of her neck. There was her hair that looked and felt like her hair, though it was strangely combed, parted on one side, not down the middle or pulled back in a clip, as she liked it. Her face was hers, though with the swelling, its angles had softened, its planes rounded, reminding me less of Fran as I'd seen her just hours before than as she was years ago when she was pregnant. Her eyes were closed. She looked neither calm nor troubled. Her skin, where it wasn't bruised, had a yellow tinge, like the color of smokers' fingers. She still wore her skirt and her maroon sweater that nipped in at her waist.

"For the record," the man said, "is this your wife, Frances Finley?

I said yes, and when he'd ushered me out, Nat asked me, "Can I see her?"

"She looks different."

"I still want to see her."

So I said okay, and, taking her hand, we went through the door and into the room, where in her usual jeans and pea jacket, she stood frightened and looked at Fran, while my eyes fixed on Nat's long, narrow legs and all they'd have to carry. Never had I seen, nor do I hope to ever see again, anyone so vulnerable and brave.

After I'd signed some papers—no burial, I chose cremation—Jim took us back to the inn about eleven, with Fran's wallet and folded coat on my lap, her other clothes in a grocery bag, and her wedding ring in a tiny Ziploc bag in my pocket. By then, word had spread up and down the lake. The phone was ringing. Year-Rounders were arriving. People were everywhere. *Where have they all come from? How will I feed them? Are the bathrooms cleaned?*

In the kitchen I made a list. One thing at a time:

Call Nat's school.
Wash her clothes.
Call the board of directors.
Buy eggs, coffee, bread, cold cuts.
Clean the bathrooms.

But that day I couldn't do anything on that list. Others, like the Wagoners, or Abby, who'd driven up from Little Falls where she was working as a receptionist, took care of the things on my list and started making lists of their own. They gently asked questions and helped organize. In a fog, I just said yes, that would be fine, or no, let's not do that. Then they made phone calls, ran off and returned with packages, flowers, and food. Always flowers and food. Half the women in the Adirondacks must have run to their ovens the second they heard the news. Pies, fruitcakes, chili, and every casserole you can imagine appeared on all the kitchen counters and sometimes outside the porch door where I'd trip over them. *How are we going to eat all this?*

Soon my parents arrived and made themselves useful. I recall my mother sitting for hours on the annex stairs with Nat, just holding her hand. Or standing in an apron, stirring soup on the stove. And my father in his poplin jacket and khakis, actually sweeping the porch. Or cleaning the bathroom on his hands and knees. Somehow that brought me to tears. I'd never seen him on his knees, working like that before.

The next day, Fran's parents' Volvo crept down the driveway. I could hardly make myself go out to meet them. What could I say? How could I explain? In the past year, her father, who'd always been a dynamo, had undergone surgery for a broken hip, and now her mother did the driving. They didn't seem to want to get out of the car, and when they finally did, they barely spoke, or couldn't speak, and neither of them would look me in the face. Gaunt and stricken, Fran's mother rushed by me and hugged Nat with such fierceness that Nat was frightened and tried to pull away. Fran's father wouldn't come inside for a while, but stood on the knoll in his brown fedora and black overcoat, leaning on his cane as if he might fall over, not turning his gaze from the ice-capped mountain. He seemed so suddenly old.

I can't remember the details of how it was all pulled together, or even many details of the event itself, but three days after the accident, we had a memorial service in the living room, with Fran's ashes in a baby-blue box, the size of a shoe box, on the mantelpiece. *That* filled my mind. It was astounding. *How could she possibly fit in there? She didn't even like that shade of blue. "A little girl's color," she'd have called it. Not Fran at all.* Someday, I figured, we'd have a good laugh about this, after she'd come back from wherever she'd gone, her arms full of mail or groceries, pushing the door open with her knee.

I have a slightly better memory of everyone milling around during the reception later. I recall my mother with her arm around Fran's mother's waist for a time, and our fathers sitting silently, side by side, on the living room sofa. I was stunned to see Howie Sanders, our teaching buddy from back at Garfield High. After his particularly unpleasant visit following our move here, Fran and I had drifted apart from him, and we hadn't corresponded in years. Yet there he was in a brown suit and tie, married, with thinning hair, a different job, but still wearing some version of his cockeyed wire-rim glasses. And there were his eyes, with such hurt and sympathy in them, as if suddenly all the years didn't matter, and the three of us, he, Fran, and I, were drinking beers in our basement apartment in Clifton, lost, beginning teachers again.

Now all around Nat and me were people, like Abby, in tears. People who touched our elbows or embraced us, like Orma, with her single, good, hammerlock of an arm, and who smelled like Fells Naptha. There were people who kept looking at us, and people who couldn't look. There were people who just talked and talked, and others, like Jim Owen, who were speechless. Numbers of folks offered help. To replace the van, Roddy Houk, from the NAPA store, said I could have one of his old pickup trucks for free, if I could put a battery in it and drive it out of the weeds behind his shed—"You'd be doing me a favor." From Mr. Blake, in his early sixties now, I learned that I was welcome to continue working here for as long as I wanted. He laid one hand on my shoulder and with the other pressed a check into my palm. He said that the members of the board would provide funds for me to hire someone part-time to do many of Fran's usual jobs. If, on the other hand, I wanted to leave in the near future, they wouldn't hold me to the contract we'd recently signed. They thought it wise for the inn to accept no reservations for November. Few guests were likely to be here anyway. I'd need some time off. Time to think. Time to adjust. Then I could "play it by ear" for a number of months. I could see how things worked out.

While people swirled about us, Nat and I tried to keep each other in sight. Gone was all her teenage brashness, gone even her eyeliner and shredded jeans. Pale and ghostly in a beige sweater and gray pants, she followed me, then I followed her, her face so blank and bewildered, as though she didn't know where she was.

Four days later, my parents left after helping to clean up and deal with the mind-boggling paperwork: the death certificate, social security, the credit cards, insurance—all the forms that needed to be signed, all of which rammed home the idea, *Yes, this must have actually happened.*

The following afternoon, Fran's parents were the last to leave. For most of their time here, they'd stayed in their room or gone for short, gimpy walks on the knoll, or had eaten alone at the table for two in the corner of the dining room. We'd barely spoken. I don't think they wanted company, and I had the feeling that, though they didn't say it, they held me responsible for not keeping their daughter safe.

At the door, Fran's mother hugged Nat fiercely again. When she'd let go, and as Nat watched from the porch, I walked with Fran's parents, carrying their luggage to their car. I brushed leaves off their wipers. I offered to help Fran's father get into the passenger seat, but despite his evident discomfort, he wouldn't let me open his door or hold his elbow. When he'd settled himself in the car, he sat with his cane beside him, his head bowed, and his hat on his lap.

Fran's mother just stood by her open door. Reluctant to get out of the car when they'd arrived, she seemed reluctant now to get in. Gathering herself the way Fran would do, she straightened her back and held her eyes on me. "Mark, will you do something for us, and for Nat, as well? Will you think about coming back?" "Home," she added. "You and Nat would be near us and your parents and old friends." She turned her gaze toward the lake. "This is all very beautiful, but it's no place for a girl without a mother, especially at this time in her life. Will you think about that? Please?"

I said thanks, yes, I would. I told them that in the meantime they were always welcome here. I said we'd always be family, something that was more true and complex than I could have grasped at the time, and something that I haven't fully grasped yet and perhaps never will. Without Fran, was I still a son-in-law? Without her, were her parents still parents anymore? Without her, was I still even married? A husband? I couldn't fathom any of this.

Then they were gone, and I walked back from the parking lot and stood on the porch with Nat. We were huddled in our coats. It was almost dusk. A breeze had started up, and we could hear a branch scraping the tin roof and then the faint honking of Canada geese way up in the sky. They, too, were heading south. We went inside. All the sofas and armchairs were empty. No one was talking and cleaning up in the kitchen. Water wasn't rushing through pipes in the walls. No floorboards creaked above. Even the mice were silent.

Nat hung her coat on a peg across from the reception desk, right next to Fran's down jacket. Then Nat's face, everything that she'd held together for days, collapsed and fell into pieces. Crying, she ran through the kitchen and up the annex stairs to her room, while I followed. The whole inn seemed to heave with her sobs.

How will I raise this kid on my own?

15

I still don't know if it was the best thing for her: I didn't force Nat to go to school. I didn't have the heart for it. The day after Fran's funeral, Nat didn't want me to take her to the bus stop. She wouldn't go the next day and the day after that, and, without us saying much about it, her staying home became routine. At first, a few friends called her, but soon those calls petered out. She lost weight, if you can imagine that. I could almost see her shedding it, her cheeks hollowing, her shoulders sagging. She seemed at once to be aging and regressing. Most days, she wore the same loose flannel shirt and baggy, mud-colored cargo pants that dragged on the floor. Her hair hung around her face like weeds. At meals, she pushed food back and forth across her plate. Sometimes, she'd cry out in her sleep, and I'd go in her bedroom and she'd let me rub her back. Those nights, she seemed like an infant again, while in daylight she was unlike any teenager I've ever known or heard of. Though I'd hired Mabel Page, a kind woman in her sixties, to begin part-time housekeeping when our guests would return in December, Nat, on her own, silently started doing jobs at the inn. She unhooked the living room curtains, washed, ironed, and rehung them. She vacuumed the guest rooms upstairs, and the next day, though no one had been in them, she vacuumed them again. One afternoon, I found her in the kitchen boiling applesauce and sealing it in mason jars, just as Fran would do.

"Honey," I said as gently as I could, "you don't have to do all that."

"Are you telling me I can't help? I can't handle this?" she asked, tears rimming her eyes.

"No, of course not."

"Then why do you want that old lady coming here? Who needs her?"

"Look, I'm just saying . . ."

But I didn't know what I was saying. Was I saying that Nat couldn't be like Fran? Or that she couldn't take some comfort in doing her mother's familiar jobs? Or that it pained me too much when she reminded me of Fran? But when *wouldn't* she remind me? Or was I saying that I simply couldn't handle any of this and I just wanted it all to stop?

In any case, I didn't have the wit or words. I didn't know what I was feeling. I didn't know what I was doing. So I let Nat do what she wanted, and she wanted to stay home. Of course, the high school's counselor called. Repeatedly, I put off his concerns, though I knew Nat was pulling inward and away from her classmates and needed to get back to school. The truth is that in those early weeks after Fran's death, I liked Nat being nearby, her *presence*, the humming of the vacuum in the hall, the sweet smell of apples boiling on the stove. A week after the first hard frost, she cut down the perennials, and toward mid-November, she repainted one of our guest rooms. From the doorway, I watched her in a work shirt and a pair of old jeans. She was standing on a canvas drop cloth, furiously pushing the roller up and down on the walls, as sprinkles of paint, like a mist, caught in the fine hairs on her arms. Lamps blazed all over. The whole room seemed to hang with humidity, and the finished walls shone a creamy yellow, smooth and soft as butter.

"It's beautiful!" I said.

She didn't say anything, didn't seem to hear me. She just kept painting, her thin arms going like pistons, as if her will and a coat of paint could change more than the surface of things.

On the other hand, I could barely function during much of that time. Almost anything could send me off the deep end or dissolve me and put me out of commission. Once, it was a phone call from the dentist's receptionist in Broadalbin to remind Fran of a Tuesday appointment:

"I'm afraid she'll have to cancel," I said.

"Then I'm afraid we'll have to charge our cancellation fee."

"Rot in hell!" was my useful response.

Another time it was "Crazy Bill" Hines, a local fixture, an old Vietnam vet with some mental deficits, who, while bagging my groceries, asked aloud what everyone else must have been wondering: "On that night of the car wreck, where were you driving *from*?"

"None of your Goddamn business!" I said right in the middle of the checkout aisle.

Back at the inn, I'd remember the way Fran would pull a sweater over her head, untucking her shirttails and frizzing her hair, and I'd have to lie down for an hour. Or I'd see her brush on her bureau, with strands of hair still tangled in the tines, and with that ripe, soapy smell of her scalp. Or her clothes in the closet. *Do I wash them?* I didn't touch them. Or her things in the medicine cabinet. Toothbrush, deodorant, cuticle scissors. *Would she have just left them behind?* Or the box of her ashes. *Where do I put it?* I stuck it in Fran's bureau drawer where Nat used to sleep as a baby. Or what about the sheets on our bed? *Her smell again! When do I change them?* Or that hollow, her imprint, on her side of the mattress? Or the recorded message still on the phone: Fran's urgent voice, like she was right there on the other end of the line. She *was* right there. Or *had been* right there: "Sweetie, can you hear me? We're on our way. We'll be right home. Love you."

Days and nights passed in a hazy, sleepless stupor. I was absent-minded, even more inept than when Fran and I had started working here. Luckily, no guests were around. I dropped dishes and couldn't sweep up the shards. I forgot when it was time to eat. For a while, I wouldn't even answer the phone—it seemed like too much trouble. Nor would I open the mail. A couple of times, I walked down to the boathouse, opened the door, and once inside, I couldn't remember why I'd gone there and why it had seemed so important. Any little problem felt insurmountable. One night, just a light bulb winking out in our living area upstairs . . . I didn't know what to do.

"You all right?" Nat asked, seeing me sitting motionless in the dark.

Desperately, she needed me to be normal and competent, and always I came up short. As the weeks went by, she'd get on my case about things I'd forget, or things I didn't do, or things I did but not as well as Fran, which seemed to be just about everything.

"What's wrong with you?" she asked me sharply on one particularly bad afternoon, when she saw me standing at the kitchen sink, hands in pockets, doing nothing, just gazing out at the woods through the window. As it happened, that was Fran's and my anniversary, and I was thinking about her, that look in her eye, that soft yet challenging edge in her voice, and that way she'd drag her finger across my wrist, or put her hand on her hip, or lift her chin ever so slightly when she'd say, "You feel like going up the brook?"

"What's wrong?" I said. I looked right at Nat. "Is that what you asked me? What's *wrong*?"

She glanced away and didn't say anything.

And then—though, God knows, I wish I hadn't—I lost it. "I can't believe you're asking me that! What's *wrong*? Everything! In case you haven't noticed, your mother is dead. Your bedroom's a disaster area. You dress like a slob. You hardly ever take a shower. You don't go to school. You don't go anywhere. You're probably flunking all your courses. What would your mother think about *that*?!"

"And what would she think about *you*?" Nat screamed at the top of her lungs. "You're useless! Pathetic! At least I'm doing things around here!"

In separate cars, my parents and Fran's drove up and joined us for Thanksgiving. Nat spent most of the time in her room. Fran's mother cooked in the kitchen, with me helping now and then, while my father watched football games on the TV in the living room and Fran's father, who'd managed to get himself down the cellar stairs, tinkered with some of my unfinished chores at the work bench. Meanwhile, my mother, needing something to keep herself busy, ironed everything she could get her hands on: sheets, pillowcases, napkins, dishcloths, shirts, pants, and even Nat's and my underwear. Though beneath one roof, we were each wrapped in our own private grief, and when together, we were excessively cautious with one another, as if one wrong word might open a chasm.

At dinner in the otherwise vacant dining room, no one sat at the opposite end of the table from me, which would have been Fran's place. No one knew how much, if at all, we should talk about her. She seemed to be everywhere and nowhere. To me, she even seemed to be listening.

Trying to say some sort of grace before the meal, I began, "Let's all be thankful for . . ." But I couldn't finish.

"This food," my mother said, bailing me out in her determined, chipper voice. She wore a silver pin on her collar, as she usually did on holidays. "Yes, this turkey smells wonderful!" She took a bite, and addressing herself to Fran's mother across the table, "Tell me Louise, what's your secret?"

Fran's mother seemed to take a long time to understand the question, as if it was in some strange language or as if she'd heard it faintly, from a great distance. Eventually she said, "Tinfoil." But she didn't elaborate.

"I hear that a cold front is coming through," I said, collecting myself and trying to get conversation going again.

"Yes," my mother said and was abruptly at a loss for words herself.

"Yes, a cold front . . ." Fran's mother said. "I understand that . . ." and touching her napkin to her lips, her voice trailed off into silence. She excused herself and went into the bathroom for five minutes. The clock ticked on the sideboard.

Meanwhile, my father, hunched in his rumpled old tweed jacket, ate quietly and carefully, as if not to disturb the air or his new upper palate. Fran's father barely ate at all. From my end of the table, I could hear his insides making noises, and it must have been his bad hip that made him keep shifting in his chair.

At one point, reaching for the gravy, I knocked the cranberry sauce over on the tablecloth, and both mothers leapt up, as with jolts of electricity, fetching bowls of water, sponges, paper towels, and Mr. Clean.

"It's not a toxic chemical spill!" Nat said ruefully. She was the only person under forty-nine years old at the table, and she just didn't want to be there. Inadvertently, and without any harm intended, she soon became the object of concerns and questions that her grandparents may not have been able to express to each another. "How are you managing? It must be hard." "Getting enough sleep?" "Eating well?" "Keeping up with your friends?" And once Fran's mother asked, "How's school?"

How in the world was Nat supposed to answer all that? She sat there, glum and silent, her eyes drilling holes in her plate. I saw a tiny muscle twitch at the bottom of her jaw, where her hair came down like a ragged curtain. I tried to say something on her behalf, that she "was taking a break from school," and that both of us were "just trying to keep our heads above water." Which clearly we weren't.

Without touching her pumpkin pie, Nat put down her fork and left the room. Later, as I helped both mothers clean up in the kitchen, it was *my* mother this time, who, elbow-deep in dishwater, said, "Nat's in such pain. Both of you are. You should think about moving back."

"Yes, this is when family can help out," Fran's mother put in, tying on an apron and hand-drying the dishes. "And being nearby makes a difference."

"You could stay with us, until you get your feet on the ground," my mother said. "We have that extra bedroom. There are lots of jobs you could apply for back home. The economy's booming. You could teach again. You could find a nice place with decent schools for Nat. Our district, for example, is pretty good. She could have a fresh start. She's young. If she's doing poorly, she could even repeat her senior year. I bet she'd find some good friends. You both would. Let us help."

Outmanned, or outwomanned, as I was, I said I'd think about it.

"Well, how about at least coming down for Christmas and New Year?" my mother said. "The inn's closed that week. Right?"

Again, I said I'd think about it. Meanwhile, I'd try to get back to work here. "Next week we'll have our first customers since the accident, and maybe that'll be a good thing."

Neither my mother nor Fran's said anything. They just kept washing, rinsing, and drying, something more seeming to pass between them than dishes and silverware.

"Maybe we'll get into a good working rhythm," I continued. On weekend mornings, I'd set a fire, make coffee, mix juice, and put out a continental breakfast for guests. I'd clean up when they were done. On those afternoons, Mabel would come, strip beds, and cook dinner, while I'd shovel snow or work on inside jobs. Nat, I hoped, would pitch in when she could. We had an inn to run, guests to serve. "Maybe that will give us something else to focus on, something else to do with our time."

"Maybe," my mother said doubtfully.

Guests did arrive, a few of them, after the beginning of December, the first being a family of four, including two preschoolers, who'd reserved a room for a three-day weekend. Though friends of some Regulars, the parents were brand new to the inn. They'd never known Fran, and that may have made it easier at first. Around noon on Friday, I took their bags and showed them to their room. I offered tea, coffee, hot chocolate, and milk. I made small talk about our first four or five inches of snow and how peaceful and still it was at that time of year—the lake was just freezing over. All this I could do without mentioning Fran and having to make any explanations. In the living room, they read magazines and did jigsaw puzzles, as Nat, who had a warm spot for children, played with their kids on the rug, building houses with Legos and Lincoln Logs.

But when unsuspecting Mabel, in her printed dress and tan support stockings, bustled in for her first afternoon of work, Nat dropped the toys, cried "Oh, my God!" and raced up to her room. This startled the kids and disturbed the parents. "What's going on?" they asked. Caught up in some strange drama they hadn't bargained for, they brought down their luggage the next morning and, without quite meeting my eyes, checked out two days earlier than planned.

Whenever Mable came, Nat ran to her room like that and wouldn't come out until hours after Mabel had left, and now she wouldn't do any of those jobs around the inn that she'd insisted on doing just weeks before. No vacuuming or dusting. Certainly no rolling paint on walls. No applesauce simmering on the stove. One afternoon when Mabel was here, I didn't hear Nat moving around upstairs, so I went to check on her. In her room, the curtains were drawn, but she wasn't napping on her bed. Nor was she slouched in her chair or sprawled amid all the stuff on her rug, reading or listening to music. Eventually, I opened her closet, and there she was in that small, slope-ceilinged storage area behind her shoes and a pile of dirty clothes. I got down on my knees and held her. She was curled up, shaking like a scared kitten, a child of the shadows again.

Meanwhile, the phone calls came every few nights from New Jersey, mostly from my mother, though I had the feeling she was speaking for Fran's parents, as well. One call I remember went like this:

"How are things going?"

"About as well as you'd expect," I said. "We've had some guests the last few days. Our first cross-country skiers."

"That's good. How's Nat faring?"

"So-so. We're trying to get back to something like normal. I just got a Christmas tree."

"We're gearing up for the holidays, too." There was an awkward silence, and my mother went on, "The other day at Shop Rite, I ran into your old teaching pal Howie. Turns out he lives nearby. Mark, have you gotten Nat back to school yet?"

"Not yet."

Another pause. "Don't forget we're just a half hour from the city now," she said. "Remember how you liked it when you were a kid. Rockefeller Center. Skating. Nat might like that too."

At the moment, I couldn't imagine Nat skating to the strains of "Holly, Jolly Christmas," and I couldn't bear the thought of my parents or Fran's seeing either of us just then and particularly Nat, who was even more edgy and withdrawn than when they'd last seen her. "She might like it," I replied, "but I think we're going to stay here for the holidays. I'm sorry. We need to work things out ourselves, the two of us."

I had, in fact, gotten a Christmas tree, as I'd always done around the third week of December. I'd managed to get myself out in the woods, where I chopped down a six foot balsam. I hauled it back, stood it in a stewpot of water in front of the living room window, and one snowy evening after Mabel had left and our few guests had gone to bed early, Nat came downstairs and into the living room in that tentative, almost soundless way of hers. She was barefoot and in her nightgown.

"Shall we trim it?" I asked.

"All right." Certainly not a resounding "Yes!" but not a "No" either.

From the storage room in the basement, I got the big box containing the strung-together lights and the ornaments. I started arranging the lights at the top, and then slowly, taking more care than me, Nat joined in, draping them around the rest of the tree. One by one, we unwrapped the fragile glass balls from the crepe paper that all three of us, including Fran, had packed them in the year before. Nat and I hung them on the boughs. We didn't say a word. Now and then she stepped back, studied the tree, then moved an ornament an inch this way or that. Like Fran, she liked to organize things—some things anyway.

When we were done, I said it was "the best tree we've ever had," which is what I've said and meant every year. And standing there, with the smell of balsam, our fingers sticky with sap, and with the glow of the lights on Nat's face if not in her eyes, it seemed that we might be more normal again. Eventually. Sometime.

A few nights later, on Christmas Eve, when the inn again was all ours, Nat put a small, wrapped present for me under the tree, which she must have ordered from a catalogue, as she hadn't left the inn. I hung Nat's stocking, a wool sock, over the fireplace. As always, I'd fill it later that night, and in the morning, after breakfast, she'd pull out its contents.

"Let's try to have a good day tomorrow." I said. "I'll put on that green plaid shirt you gave me last year. I'll make bacon, eggs, and muffins. Why don't you wear something nice? Let's enjoy some little things. I think Mom would want us to do that."

We said goodnight. After she'd gone up to her room, I stuffed her stocking with fruit and candy. On the hearth, I put the wrapped box containing the leather, fleece-lined boots I'd bought for Nat down in Amsterdam. I thought they'd be warm and look good on her whenever she'd go back to school. Then, after I switched off the lights on the tree, I went up to bed myself.

As a little kid, Nat was always the first awake on Christmas morning, but in the last few years, it had always been me or Fran, and it was me again this time, because, with the wind rattling the bedroom window—and with everything else that kept rattling inside me—I had never really gotten to sleep. I got dressed in that green shirt and a fresh pair of pants. Downstairs, I opened the curtains, and through grills of icicles hanging from the gutters, I could see the lake sprawled out there, all frozen and white. Lately, we'd had a cold snap, and that night, our first heavy snowfall. In the kitchen, I started the oven, greased the muffin tins, and mixed up batter. Soon I heard Nat moving around upstairs, the floorboards creaking, the shower running, and the water whooshing through the pipe in the wall beside the stove. I heard the shower turn off as I poured out the batter and put the tins in the oven. A few moments later, some lights blinked, which meant Nat was running the hair drier. As I fried bacon, I heard her moving up there again, and when it was cooked, I went back in the living room and waited for her to come down.

I was facing the tree and the window, when I heard her step into the room. I turned. And what I saw was . . . *Fran?*

Nat was looking straight at me. She wore a plain, spruce-colored dress of Fran's with the red cardigan sweater that Fran always wore on

Christmas, the one with ribbing around the waist and, around the collar, big embroidered snowflakes that seemed to have fallen there. Nat's hair was shining, combed, and pulled back neatly behind her ears. She was beautiful in her thin, evanescent way, and she just stood there with her face and eyes wide open, as if waiting for me to say or do something, to go to her and throw my arms around her.

But I didn't. Shaken, I turned back to the window. I couldn't look at her. I thought of Nat upstairs in Fran's closet, leafing through clothes on hooks and hangers, holding them in front of herself at the mirror, gathering a cream-colored camisole to her face, and breathing in, the smell of salt and talcum powder. And then trying on different outfits, stepping into pants, slips and skirts, buttoning blouses, pulling on sweaters, the feel of them sliding over her skin. Wool, terry cloth, silk, denim. Her feet slipping into Fran's flat, black shoes. Was it comforting? Familiar? Horrifying? Bewildering?

When I finally turned back to her, Nat must have seen the pain and confusion in my face, because I could see it now in hers. She looked at me desperately, her eyes like bulbs, her hands fluttering at her sides. "I thought you'd like it!" she said. "I thought . . ."

I still couldn't move.

Then she kicked off the shoes, ripped off the sweater, and threw it down. Weeping, bent over as with a pain in her chest, she turned and ran back through the kitchen and up the stairs.

And worse, I didn't go to help her. Worse yet, I didn't want to touch her. I didn't even want to be near her. I smelled the muffins burning.

Moments later, I went to the kitchen, turned off the oven, and pulled out the smoking muffins. All were charred, gone.

Then for some reason that I still don't understand—maybe I just had to get out of there, *away*—I put on my heavy coat and shoved my feet into boots. Outside, about eight inches of snow had mounded up, and while I knew it marked the beginning of another long, hard, bleak winter, it still had that transforming newness, tall and balanced along the tops of branches, even along the narrowest twigs, making the woods along the edges of the knoll so fragile-looking, like calligraphy. I didn't think to get skis or snow shoes from the basement. Kicking snow ahead of me, I walked out across the knoll, ran and slid down the hill, through the field where grasses lay buried in white humps, until I reached the boat-house. What did I think I was doing? Going out for a morning row on the frozen lake? I don't think I was thinking at all. When I pulled open the door, it swept a fan in the snow. Inside, it was dim but not dark. My eyes took a moment to adjust. It was all so different than in other seasons, when swallows swoop and water laps against the creaking dock. Now everything was still and quiet. No smells of waterlogged boards or muddy nests. While open to the lake on the far side, there wasn't any snow in there. Just glare ice, dark and thick as granite. And in its grip, the guide-boat.

How could I have forgotten?

People who live around northern lakes know how ice expands, how it buckles upward in steep ridges or downward in folds, the whole frozen surface of the lake pushing outward against its shores, sometimes with hundreds of pounds of pressure per square foot. Large boulders are shoved around. Breakwaters get broken. Docks, as I've mentioned, are tilted and twisted. Battered each winter, the shore each spring is not what it was in the fall.

I should have stepped inside and onto the dock to take a closer look. Then I should have gone up to the woodshed and grabbed the ax. I should have returned, and, because it would only thicken with time, its pressure increasing, I should have bashed at the ice with all my might, until I'd freed the boat, whatever its condition, and winched it into the air.

But I'd come to a time when I couldn't deal with these broken things anymore. There were too many of them. I couldn't fix them. I didn't have the strength. I couldn't hold them in my mind. I didn't even want to know about them. So I turned and, closing it behind me, went out the door and left the boat to the ice.

Back up at the inn and upstairs in our apartment, I heard Nat still crying quietly behind her closed door. I went to the phone. With the receiver shaking in my hand, I called my mother. How many times had Nat done this, called or *called out* to *her* mother, but without an answer?

I heard my mother's voice on the phone. She was calm. She seemed to expect to hear from me and knew exactly what I was thinking. "You coming?"

"Yes. We'll be down there soon. This evening."

I know it's a cliché, but it's true: a change of place can change your mind.

After I'd put down the phone, I knocked softly on Nat's door, and a moment later she let me in. Her eyes were hollow, dry now, though strands of her hair were still dark and wet with tears. Already she was out of Fran's clothes and back in her usual flannel shirt and baggy pants.

"I think we should get out of here for a while," I said. "It might do us some good."

She agreed, and silently at the kitchen table, we ate the remains of breakfast, the bacon, eggs, and some bread I toasted to replace the muffins. Still silently, we cleaned up and packed our suitcases. I plowed the driveway with the tractor. Back inside, I phoned Mabel, asking her to check the inn while we'd be gone, and I arranged for Bruce Wagoner to do any more needed plowing with his Bronco. As if they'd somehow understood, neither of them asked why we were leaving so suddenly, and on Christmas morning. They both said not to worry about things up here.

I grabbed the stocking and boxes from the hearth. At the thermostat, I turned the heat down to fifty, then switched off most of the lights. Luckily, the pickup had a full tank of gas, and soon we were the only moving vehicle for miles, first on the plowed dirt road, then turning onto Route 8, passing Orma's, Stephenson's, the clinic, and the market in Speculator, all with their parking lots snow-covered, without tire tracks, like flat, empty fields. On Route 30, we passed the Cedar View and the Sea Horse with the flickering "No" preceding "Vacancy" lit up on the neon sign, though there wasn't a car there, either. Everyone was at home, indoors, the whole world shut down for the day.

As we headed further south, the low mountains fell away in my rearview mirror, and smoke curled from the stove pipes of occasional houses and trailer homes. Going down the big hill in Amsterdam at noon, we left the fresh snow behind us, and I was surprised by how much else we seemed to be leaving behind. On the Thruway, we sped east along the Mohawk and parts of the old Erie Canal, then turned south again at Albany. Now we were moving against the flow of pioneers and western expansion, against the flow of history, the country's, and our own. By the time we hit the Jersey state line a few hours later, I wasn't even thinking about burned muffins or the pressure of lake ice, and Nat was actually listening to Christmas carols that came in with amazing clarity on the radio.

At their condo in Caldwell, my mother, as always, had prepared and decorated to the hilt. She wore a red skirt for our arrival, and my father, no doubt under my mother's direction, had put on a red vest and even kissed Nat, who didn't flinch, under the mistletoe. In the living room, sprigs of holly garnished every surface. Pine swags festooned the windows. A huge, stuffed kneesock with Nat's name on it hung over the fireplace, and their Christmas tree seemed to levitate over a mountain of gifts, each wrapped in matching glossy green paper and done up with a silver bow. How had my mother been so sure we'd be coming? Nat couldn't keep her eyes off the presents.

Soon Fran's parents arrived. Her mother greeted both of us warmly, and her father vigorously shook my hand and wanted to know all about our trip. They were parents who'd lost their only child, a circumstance I simply couldn't imagine, and you could see the pain in the crinkles around their eyes, but they were determined to be cheerful.

At dinner, conversation never lagged, everyone pitching in like teammates, and afterward Nat was literally showered with gifts. From Fran's parents, she got a bathrobe, bracelets, and a big, floppy purse, things that Fran might have thought of. Among a myriad of other presents, my parents gave her a leather-bound diary and a beautiful cherrywood recipe box, already crammed with enough recipes to keep Nat busy for months. Nat gave me the *National Geographic Pocket Guide to Birds of North America* and the *Audubon Society Pocket Guide to Familiar Trees*, "so you'll know what you're looking at," she said. I gave her the fleece-lined boots. Immediately, she slid her feet into them and, even if only for a second, put her arms around me to say thanks.

Then began five days of wall-to-wall planned activities. They were right there, inscribed in my mother's neat printing on her kitchen calendar. We all took the train into New York and stood on a long line to see the window displays at Macy's, and we watched the crush of skaters at Rockefeller Center. On another day, we saw the Nutcracker at the Paper Mill Playhouse in Millburn and raced through the Newark Museum before our parking meter expired. We spent most of another afternoon walking the grounds of Caldwell High School and, with our faces pressed to the glass, peering in all the wide windows. Never had Nat seen a school with so many amenities: a full-sized gym, a library with cushy lounge chairs, classrooms with computers at every desk, and—this really lit up her eyes—a pool. They had a swimming team!

Next on the docket was an afternoon of shopping with Fran's mother. And on the second to last day of the year, while Nat and my mother dug into that recipe box and made cookies, Howie Sanders squired me around some neighborhoods "just to get a feel for" the local real estate and rental markets. When Howie had left teaching, and, with his flair for dramatic overstatement, had fit right into advertising, he'd landed at a company in West Orange, where he'd met Barbara, who had a daughter from a previous marriage. He told me there were good jobs all over North Jersey, new businesses springing up. Later that day, I drove Nat over to Howie's handsome brick colonial, where he introduced us to Barb and then to their daughter Lisa and a girlfriend, both of whom were seniors, in the same grade as Nat but years more sophisticated in their makeup, short skirts, black tights, and with their pink cell phones ever-ready in their hands. The girls were friendly, bubbling with pheromones, and they invited Nat to go with them to the Livingston Mall to see a movie that was in fact "just released," as opposed to every other movie Nat had ever seen.

Of course Nat wanted to go, and while she was there, Howie, Barb, and I went to a nearby Mexican restaurant where some of Fran's and my old friends and their acquaintances joined us, most of whom, like Howie, had moved from teaching to other careers and were now married with families. One of the women that I didn't know, however, seemed unattached to a spouse, and I had the awkward but not altogether disagreeable feeling that our meeting had been arranged.

Her name was Joanne, and she appeared to be in her late thirties. She had straight, shiny black hair, cut on an angle just below her ears and above the collar of her camel's hair coat, a look that I would call more "crisp" than either "hard" or "severe." Her face was thoughtful, her eyes dark and almond-shaped. After she'd hung her coat on a hook near mine, we took our places opposite one another at the long table. She had a way of sitting so her back didn't touch the chair and a way of listening intently and speaking precisely and clearly, as though making sure she was not misunderstood. She referred with pleasure to her "live wire" nine-year-old son who was with a pal for dinner, and she referred with less pleasure to the boy's "father," but never to a "husband."

Before anyone had even mentioned it, she seemed aware of what had happened to Fran. "I'm sorry about your wife's death," she said, looking steadily at me, as if she had some sense of this kind of loss. Her hands were small, smooth-looking, without nail polish or rings, and when she spoke they were very still. Over a white blouse, she wore a short, tailored brown jacket. A simple copper bracelet circled her left wrist. For some years, she'd been the head nurse on the pediatrics floor at Morristown Memorial Hospital, she said, and she struck me as the kind of warm and earnest person who, in the face of some longstanding difficulty, had made a hard-earned life for herself and her son, a life more contained than she might have anticipated, but one that she could be proud of.

As the margaritas and food went around the table, we all spoke over the piped-in mariachi music in that pleasant, if superficial, way of friends who haven't been in touch for many years. I talked about the lake, the hills, and my work as an innkeeper. There were toasts to Fran, and then some good-natured ribbing and jokes about how we all seemed to be aging, "though not maturing," and I realized that this was my first night out since Fran had died, and I felt both good and bad about it. I was enjoying myself, but without her. Somehow it seemed that I'd left her back at the inn, cleaning up after dinner, dealing with a guest's complaint or some other problem, and here I was sitting and talking amiably in another place with an attractive woman who wasn't like Fran at all. The whole thing was very weird, and sometimes I relished all the good cheer, and then suddenly it seemed oppressive and relentless.

At one point, excusing myself, I got up and, grabbing my coat along the way, went down the narrow hall past the rest rooms, the kitchen, and out through the back door for some fresh air. This was where trucks unloaded big sacks of rice on wooden pallets, and where the cooks and wait staff must come for a smoke—cigarette butts littered the pavement. Beyond a chain-link fence, the lights of cars came in waves along South Orange Avenue. I could hear a plane circling for Newark airport. The breeze was sharp and cold and smelled of onions and refried beans. An exhaust fan whirred in the wall beside me. So much for my fresh air.

After a time, I heard the door open behind me. I turned with an uneasy flicker of anticipation, and yes, it was Joanne, walking out in her jacket and creased pants, but not in her heavy coat. She was rubbing her hands together, then wrapping her arms around herself as she came near.

"I was wondering where you'd gotten to," she said in her calm way and fixing me with her eyes. Then she stood next to me, shoulder to shoulder, and said, "You okay?"

I nodded. "Thanks. And you?"

"Cold. But okay."

She looked up at the sky, and I had the feeling that she was as tired from the holiday festivities as I was. She said, "It must be strange for you, all this." She let out a breath and continued, "Relief from your kind of pain, I imagine, must be pretty disorienting."

I nodded and said it was. For a moment, I didn't know what else to say, so again I said, "Thanks." Then I said, "I suppose there're all kinds of disorienting pain. I doubt I have a monopoly on it."

She said yes, then tipped her head back at a different angle and seemed to change the subject. "The stars, they're about as clear as they ever get around here. I bet you can see the Milky Way up north where you live."

"A fair bit of it," I said. "You can really see it in the late summer, when the sky is jet black. It's like a swath of sky is powdered with stars. On a calm night, it's reflected in the lake. So I guess you could say you can swim in the stars."

She didn't say anything but seemed to be imagining it all. And then I was imagining *her*, swimming out there in the silvery dark, her smooth arms glinting with that light.

"Want to borrow my coat?" It just blurted out of me, and I was surprised by how easy it was to say.

"That's kind, but no thanks. I'm all right."

A busboy in a soiled apron carried garbage to a Dumpster and went back in through the door.

We were looking up again at the sky, when I felt Joanne lean her shoulder, light as a leaf, against mine. I couldn't tell if she was gently supporting herself, or me, or both of us. I didn't move. I didn't lean back against her or put my arm around her. But nor did I pull away, which I guess, as the moments passed, became a form of acceptance, an act in itself. I wanted those moments to keep going. I wanted us to stay right there. Where our shoulders touched, I could feel the lift and fall of her breathing, more slow and steady than mine, and I bet she could feel my breathing too.

For a while, we stayed like that, touching, barely moving, our breath coming out in plumes, and then I felt her shiver.

"I'm afraid I'm getting goose bumps," she said. "I have to go back in." As she straightened up, I couldn't feel her shoulder nor her breathing anymore. She went back into the restaurant.

When I'd returned there four or five minutes later, I was surprised that Joanne wasn't at the table, and her camel's hair coat wasn't hanging from the hook.

"You okay?" Howie asked, studying my face, the second person who'd said that in the last ten minutes. I must have looked distraught.

"I'm fine. It's been a long day. Should we get our kids from the movies?"

"Soon," he said, looking at his watch. "Let's have dessert first. By the way, Joanne got a phone call just before you came in. She had to go pick up her son."

That explained her absence, but I was still disappointed. I sat, picked up my napkin, and, putting it in my lap, I felt something wrapped inside it. It was a business card, and printed on it was the name and address of the hospital where Joanne worked, her own name with RN, MSN directly after it, a work phone number immediately below that, and in the lower left hand corner was another phone number and an email address written in neat, blue longhand.

Feeling that flicker of anticipation again, I slid the card into my pocket.

Later, as I drove Nat back to my parents' condo, she talked a mile a minute about all the stores in the mall, the cell phones at T-Mobile, the cool clothes at some place called Aeropostale, the lattes at Starbucks, and how much fun it was to hang out with Lisa and her friend and a few others who had joined them. She said nothing about the movie. She smelled of cigarettes and spilled beer, so I figured that after a tour of the mall, they'd bought six-packs someplace and gone somewhere else, but I didn't ask her about it. What was the use, when she was revved and chatting away so happily? Besides, I didn't have the energy to battle it out with her then.

She paused for a moment, and I could see her mood changing. I suspect she was thinking about the fast-approaching end of our visit. Right out of the blue, she said, "Lisa said we might move down here."

"Oh?"

"Yes. Her dad told her. He said you were thinking about it. Are you?"

I steered into the driveway of the condo and parked. "Maybe. I'll see."

"I'll see?" she mimicked, suddenly irked. "Do *I* have a say in this? Or is it all about *you*?"

Before I could answer, though, she'd turned away in a huff and already was out the door of the pickup.

17

On our drive back north on New Year's Day, Nat and I hit snow even before we'd left New Jersey, up near the Wanaque reservoir. It got worse as we skirted the Catskills, and worse yet as we turned west from Albany and slowly followed the plows and gritty salt trucks. The cheer of the past week evaporated. We didn't listen to the radio. We hardly spoke. The wipers, streaking, slapped back and forth. The snow came at us in streaming, mesmerizing curves, and eventually, eight hours into our five-hour trip, we pulled down the inn's driveway about dusk, surrounded by mounds of whiteness a few feet higher than when we'd left.

The next morning, I was surprised when Nat got up early, made herself breakfast, put on her coat, new boots, backpack, and asked me to drive her to the bus stop. She wanted to return to school. She was afraid of "falling too far behind," she said, then added, "either here, or, if we move, down there." So it wasn't with a sudden thirst for learning that she went back to school, but with a kind of grim determination. She'd had a vision of a life elsewhere—and friends elsewhere, and she wanted to keep pace with them.

In the next weeks, the slate sky pressed down, and snow climbed up the living room windows, like sand in the bottom of an hourglass. Though Nat went to school, we fell back into many of our old routines. When we had guests, mainly skiers and snowmobilers, I did the bare minimum. I put out breakfast, plowed, shoveled, and brought in firewood. I didn't chat with guests at happy hour. I puttered in the basement, but got little done. I didn't go near the boathouse and the guide-boat, which was still locked in ice. Nor did I go out to any potluck dinners. I didn't even call the Wagoners, and when they called, I said that we were too busy, and no thanks, we didn't need anything or feel like having company.

For me, the only small relief in those weeks were my emails back and forth with Joanne. They were neither numerous, nor long, but I remember every one. I wrote her saying that I'd enjoyed meeting her. A day later, she wrote back, "It was a pleasure. Keep me posted. Warm regards, J." In another email, I described a few of our quirky guests and, of course, the rotten weather. She told me about her demanding job and some of the sick children on her floor of the hospital, and it struck me how good and necessary her work was, and I told her that. In her next message, she thanked me for reminding her—"Sometimes I forget the important things"—and she wrote that I should let her know whenever I'd be going south again and revisiting their "more temperate zone." Reading her words, I'd think of her hands, how still they were whenever she spoke, or how, when she moved them, say, to pass the bread basket or the water pitcher, that copper bracelet would slide on her wrist.

Meanwhile, as the days passed, Nat retreated more and more into her room after school, coming out only on special occasions to complain, argue, or eat with her elbows planted on the table, shoulders slumped, and her hair hanging in her food.

"Do you really like *wearing* that spaghetti sauce?" I couldn't help myself from asking her once. On another evening, having resolved during the day to broach the subject, I suggested that I take her to see a therapist in Albany who might help her feel better.

She glanced at me as though I barely existed, sighed, shook her head, then slumped even further.

About that time, I began to find an alarming number of long, spiraling strands of her hair on the bathroom floor, and then on her bedside table, when I'd go in there while she was at school. I picked some of them up. Each ended with a tiny dab of dried blood at the bulb-shaped root. Was she pulling it out, that beautiful, reddish-brown hair? In the corner of my eye, on a couple of our trips to the bus stop, I had seen her twirling it nervously, or running her fingers along her hairline, before dropping her hands abruptly to her lap, as if she was trying to stop herself.

I mentioned the hair on the bathroom floor and again suggested the therapist.

"I don't need a therapist," she said after a long, sullen silence. We were eating supper at the kitchen table. "What I need is to get out of here. Why are we staying?"

"Nat, we just can't up and leave."

"Why not?"

"I have a job. I work here."

"Aren't there jobs in New Jersey?"

She had point. I didn't say anything.

"So what's to stop us?" she said, exasperated. "What's keeping us here, except your stubbornness?"

"Like I said, we can't just leave. Not now."

"Then when?"

"I don't know."

"That's not an answer!"

"Look, I just don't know." My voice was rising.

"Well, what *I* know is *this*: I hate this place! It's nothing but cold and snow . . . and pain. I can't stand it!" She got up from the table. She'd barely eaten, but she was done. She raked her fingernails through her hair, then tore at it with her hands.

What could I do? I couldn't stand it either. I couldn't stand to see Nat like this, or *us* like this. So the next week, with a sudden, frantic excess of energy, I put together my resumé and sent my applications for mid-level facilities maintenance positions to a few companies that Howie and others had mentioned in northern New Jersey. I went over to the Wagoners and tried to explain what I was doing, and throwing their arms around me while choking back tears, they said if we moved, they'd miss us terribly, it was almost unimaginable, but under the circumstances I was probably doing the right thing, especially for Nat. "Yes, you should go," they said.

By the beginning of February, I'd had a few encouraging job interviews by phone and had scheduled follow up face-to-face interviews, in one case "a mere formality," I was told. Astoundingly, the position was mine if I wanted it, the Assistant Director of Buildings and Grounds at Accutechnics, on Route 287, where I'd have a small office in a garage and oversee a staff of three who mowed grass, edged and weeded gardens, mulched shrubs, raked leaves, and generally kept the fifteen acres of corporate landscape looking impressive to executives and clients. I'd be a sort of innkeeper without an inn, where again I'd be "Mr. Outside." I lined up a drive-around with an apartment agent. I heard Nat on the phone arranging some get-together with Howie's daughter Lisa. All this would happen on the weekend of Nat's birthday—unbelievably, her eighteenth—when I made sure there were no reservations. Nat would take that Thursday and Friday off from school, and from her teachers get the assignments she'd miss. We'd spend those two nights with my parents and Saturday night with Fran's, all of whom could barely contain their enthusiasm. I called Howie who said, "Terrific!" I emailed Joanne to tell her that again I'd be "heading south from the Arctic Circle," and maybe we could have coffee. She emailed right back, "Certainly! Of course! Why not make it dinner?"

Just planning that trip seemed to open a curtain, a way forward, as though some shiny, new version of ourselves had sprung into being. At meals, Nat pushed back her hair and didn't fool with it. She sat up more or less straight, I didn't nag her, and we actually engaged in conversation without insulting one another. With guests, I was downright hospitable. I topped up their coffee cups at breakfast. I discussed the relative merits of goose down and synthetic insulation. To skiers, I passed out our collection of trail maps. At happy hour, I poured glasses of wine "on the house." And looking forward, I could even imagine being a happy guest here myself.

On that Thursday morning when we packed our bags, we were in the midst of a freakish February thaw, though of course there were still feet of snow all over. The sky was overcast, everything dismal, a good day to head elsewhere. Brown snow banks surrounded most of the parking lot. Indoors, the basement was flooded, and in three of the guest rooms I'd positioned stew pots on beds and floors to catch meltwater that leaked through the roof and ceilings. From everywhere came dripping, sloshing, and gurgling sounds. We were all awash, and it wasn't even near mud season yet. In New Jersey, I remembered, a real mud season hardly existed. There February gave over to a few damp, chilly weeks in March, which were also marked by some reliably hopeful signs: grape hyacinths, snowdrops, the tips of daffodils pushing up through the ground. . . . And the next thing you know, it was baseball season.

After breakfast and cleaning up, Nat and I carried our duffle bags downstairs, put on coats, and slid into boots. I pulled the door closed behind us, and we went out to the pickup. We squeezed the bags into the luggage area behind the front seat, got in, and closed the doors. Through the windshield, and beyond the knoll, I saw the boathouse and the long dock, both still caked in snow. Beyond them: the lake, where the ice looked gray, where Fran and I had skied—or tried to—during our first winter here, and where now in the distance stood those little fishing shanties, some with pools of water around them. In a month or so, the shanties would be gone. Just that big, silver beer keg would be out there, and we'd all be dropping our five-dollar bills into the coffee can on the counter at Orma's.

I put the key in the ignition, but I couldn't turn it. It was almost a physical thing, as if I was more frozen than the lake just then.

"What's wrong?" Nat said.

"I can't do it." I couldn't tell my hand to move. Suddenly it seemed that, by turning that key, Nat and I would open some door and enter a strange room with another key in another door, which we'd open into yet a stranger room, perhaps with only the twilit shapes of unfamiliar furniture, room after room, each one getting more vague, nightmarish, and weird. . . .

"Why can't you?" Nat asked. "Do you have the right key?"

"Yes."

"Then just turn it."

"I can't."

"You *can't*?" Alarmed, she looked right at me. "Or you *won't*?"

Then I knew it in my bones: there was no shiny, new version of ourselves. "We're not going."

"Are you kidding?"

"No."

"But it's my birthday! In two days. We're celebrating down there!"

"Nat, we can't go. We're staying here."

It took a few seconds for this to sink in. "Oh, Jesus!" she cried. "I knew it!" She stomped her feet on the floor mat and dropped her face into her hands. "I knew you'd give up at the last second. I wanted to believe we'd do it, and I actually *did* believe, but it was all too good to be true! Why do I bother to hope for anything? What a disaster!"

She jumped out of the pickup, slammed the door, and walked with long, determined strides to the porch and inside. I followed about ten yards behind, trying to keep up with her. She went through the living room and the kitchen and up the stairs to the annex. I'd reached our living area when she kicked shut her bedroom door and locked herself inside.

I went to the door. "Can we talk?"

"No!"

"Let me explain."

"There's nothing to explain! What you've done—what you won't do—explains everything!" For a moment, she seemed to catch her breath. What was she doing in there? Then her voice got low and menacing: "All right, if you want something to explain, I'll give you something to explain."

She unlocked the door and with an eerie calm stepped out into the hall. She was still in her baggy pants, shirt, and boots, but had taken off her coat. She was holding her hands behind her back, like she always did as a child, but she wasn't a shy little girl now. "I know where you were," she said in that same voice, her eyes as hard as stone.

"What are you talking about?"

"I think you know."

And of course I *did* know, or I had a rapidly gathering suspicion. But I said, "No, I don't."

"I know where you were on the night of the accident."

How could *she* know? She couldn't! "We were at the Cedar View," I said. "For dinner. That's where we called you from. Remember?"

Her eyes didn't change. She kept staring like that. "No, I mean later. After the Cedar View and before you and Mom started driving home. Where were you at eleven o'clock, when you should have been here? That's what I'm talking about, and you know it!"

I couldn't answer or look at her face.

Then she took her right hand from behind her back and held it upturned, straight out toward me. Loosely balled in it were Fran's bra, her silver necklace, and my plaid scarf that we'd left at the Sea Horse in our rush to get out of there on that horrible night.

For a second, I lost my balance and had to put my hand on the wall. My voice cracked. "Where did you get those?"

"From Jimmy Phelps." Jimmy was a classmate of Nat's, the son of Clyde Phelps, who manages the Sea Horse. Sometimes Jimmy does chores there. As much as Clyde's always been a good guy, Jimmy's always had a mean streak.

"He said you were at the Sea Horse late that night," Nat went on. "I told him—I told everyone—that he was a liar, that he was starting rumors. But then he brought *these* into school. He said he found them in one of the rooms on the morning after. He said the room was a mess. He said his father had written your names in their guest book." She opened her hand and let the clothes and necklace fall to the floor between us. "He hung these through the latch of my locker. Of course I knew whose they were. Now *everyone* knows whose they were!"

When I could speak, I said, "When did you get those? How long have you had them?"

"About a month."

So for a month, she'd known this and endured it, to say nothing of enduring her gossipy classmates, on top of everything else. I was mortified. For her. For us. Even for Fran.

"You'd have killed me if I'd done anything like that," Nat said, her hands in fists at her sides. "Sneaking off to a sleazy motel. You said you were just going out to dinner. You lied! You *fucking* lied! And for this Mom is ashes?"

This struck me like a blow. And now, lashing back, *I* flew off the handle. "It wasn't me who was drunk and driving on the wrong side of the road! You want to know why we went to the Sea Horse? You want to know why we rushed home?"

She turned and ran back across the living area and flew down the stairs.

"We were in love!" I screamed after her. "With each other! With you! We were rushing home to see *you*! We were worried to death about *you*! That's *fucking* why!"

I heard her sprint across the kitchen and living room, something smashing to the floor. I heard the porch door open and slam shut. *Where the hell does she think she's going? She doesn't even have her coat.*

And then, blindly, I tore after her. Down the stairs to the kitchen, knocking aside a chair. Through the dining room, the living room, crunching the shards of a glass, kicking up the rug. Through the front door, not even closing it. Onto the porch, down the stairs, and into that dismal weather.

Where had she gone? I could see to the parking lot. She wasn't there. Through bare trees, I could see a ways up the driveway. Not there. I could see across the knoll and down to the boathouse and the lake. Not there either. For a couple of minutes, I stood still and listened. I heard my heart pounding. I heard the trickle of water in gutters and downspouts. Lots of dripping. Nothing else.

Tracks. Yes. Look for tracks, I thought. *She'd have to leave tracks.*

Then I saw them, heading around the side of the inn and disappearing into the woods. They didn't stop at the woodshed, where Nat might have found shelter. They weren't heading toward the brook. They weren't following any path. I didn't know why she'd run in that direction, except that it might be a shortcut to the road and maybe, if she could hitch a ride to Route 30, she could head south.

Following her tracks, I ran. Or tried to. As the snow was heavy, she must have been plowing as much as running, her tracks two furrows, calf deep, with clots of snow pushed aside. So while she was laboring to move forward, I, in her wake, should have been catching up. But I wasn't, or didn't seem to be. Thirty yards through the snow, I was into the woods, my breath chuffing, my legs aching, and her tracks, still empty, kept receding from me. The further I ran, the further ahead they disappeared into the gray thicket of maple, beech, and ash trees and the darker trunks of pines. For a second, I thought they might be someone else's tracks or some large-footed animal's, but there in each furrow were the prints of boots, *her* boots, her size, with zigzag treads. I should know, I bought them.

How did she stay so far ahead? *Where does she get the strength?*

Sweating like crazy under my coat, I kept slogging as fast as I could, pushing hemlock branches out of my way and stumbling through wiry witch-hobble that looped up like snares through the snow. If I couldn't outrun, then by God I'd outlast her. Near the brow of a hill, I paused to listen again. Silence. I glanced backwards and the inn was gone, swallowed up in the trees, so the whole world was just these two furrows, side-by-side, perfectly parallel, that disappeared in front of and now behind me.

I started down the other side of the hill, half jogging, half sliding, almost falling. And that's when I saw a dark smudge in the tracks ahead that soon looked like the elbow of a drainpipe, though as I reached it, it turned out to be one of Nat's boots, the left one, its front end stuck in the slushy snow. She had literally run out of her boots, at least one, and she hadn't even stopped to put it back on. I thought of her white, tender feet. *How does she keep going?* Her tracks from there forward were more ragged and wobbly, with more snow kicked aside, but they still headed straight for the road. I stopped and listened again, and this time I heard her faint, distant grunting, as sharp as mine yet higher pitched. Now I ran down the hill with even more resolve, juiced with gravity and adrenaline. I came upon the second boot lying on its side near the track, like something tossed from a moving car, but I didn't even pause to examine it. *Had it flipped off her foot as she ran, or had she kicked it off intentionally? Why?*

Then I saw her, perhaps forty yards ahead, a vague, narrow shape, there and gone and there again, bird-like, as if camouflaged among the trees. Her feet must have been frozen, and soon I could see that she was struggling, limping, leaning forward as into a gale.

"Stop!" I cried.

But she kept churning, not even looking back, her shape getting sharper and darker as I closed the space between us. She was in a shallow swale, filled with snow, the road still out of sight. *Does she think she can run to New Jersey?*

Twenty yards away, I again cried "Stop!" and again she didn't stop but, finally glancing back with wild eyes, moved with even more desperation, her legs flailing through the snow, her breath coming out in yips and groans, like a wounded animal, panting.

I closed on her. Her hair streamed back so I could almost grasp it. Her arms pumped. Her feet, in her blue ragg socks, spat bits of slush.

Then I dove, catching one of her feet in the crook of my wrist, and down she went with me. She tried to scramble up, kicking my face, arms, and shoulders, but I held on with all my might, digging my fingernails into cloth and skin. And now we were fighting—for our lives, it seemed—rolling and writhing in the snow, me clawing toward her hips and waist to keep her down, as, squirming and screaming, she beat my head with her fists and pulled my hair. I grabbed at anything I might hold, if only for a second: a pocket, her belt, a sleeved forearm, a wrist. And she bit my fingers, the meat of my left hand, anything she could reach and get her teeth and fury into, until, screaming myself—"God damn you!"—I had to let go and grab at something else.

In the end, it was weight that did it, brute, parental, smothering weight. With my chest heaving, my legs straddling and clamping hers, and my hands finally pinning her wrists, I held her to that spot of earth, that snow-packed ground, until she subsided and I subsided, both of us sweating, shivering, and sobbing, everything expended, nothing left, and finally we were just still and quiet and there.

About ten minutes later, I managed to stand. Nat lay curled and broken in the snow. What had I done? And to my own daughter, now twice wounded, grievously so, once by her mother's death and now, perhaps unforgivably, by this? What trust had I shattered? What had gotten into me? What did I think I was doing, halting our trip at the moment of leaving when everything had seemed to say *go*? Was it pure stubbornness or selfishness, my keeping her here in this lonely place where she'd never flourish and didn't want to be?

And to do it so violently? With my own hands?

What kind of father was I?

And yet at that moment, I was more certain of this than I'd been certain of anything, or certain of anything since: I couldn't leave and I couldn't let her leave. Not then. Those nightmarish rooms that I'd imagined when I couldn't turn the key in the car's ignition weren't the only things that got more vague and weird, as now I imagined them again. Nat and I, unlocking those doors and moving from room to room, also lost shape and form, became unrecognizable to each other and to ourselves. Like vapor. I *had* to hold her there.

I took off my coat and put it over her. I bent and reached down my right hand, and after a moment, she took it. She was cold and weak, shivering uncontrollably now, and, pulling her up while keeping the coat around her, I dipped my head and shoulders under her arm and held her tight to me, side to side, with my elbow locked around her waist, so I could carry most of her weight. She felt long and limp, a reedy thing. Still, she tried to move on her own, taking some of her weight on her wobbly legs. Together we turned and moved a step at a time, back through the swale and up the hill, following the tracks we had made coming down it. We gasped and had to stop to catch our breath. We didn't have the strength to speak. We passed each of Nat's boots, which we couldn't have picked up and carried, even if we'd tried. We went down the hill. As we approached the edge of the woods, the inn gradually emerged through the trees. We passed the woodshed. We made it up the porch stairs. We practically fell through the open front door, and somehow—I can't remember this part—we made it up to the annex.

There I got Nat onto her bed and peeled off her waterlogged socks. Her feet were pale, but not red, blistered, or swollen. I dried them with a towel. I wrapped her in quilts, right up to her chin. She submitted without a word. Using a warm washcloth, I rubbed away the blood smears on her face. Was it my blood? Hers? Ours? She turned away toward the wall.

Through tears, I said, "I'm sorry. I know I've hurt you terribly—in all kinds of ways. I know you don't agree, and I understand if you hate me, but this, I think, is what we have to do. I hope to God I'm right. We can't run away. We can't go anywhere else. We have to learn to live without your mom, and this is where we have to do it."

Exhausted, I sat with her until her shivering stopped and she fell asleep.

18

You can never really tell about the paths that you chose not to take, whether they'd have turned out better or worse than the ones you actually took. Would Fran's life and mine have been better if long ago we hadn't moved from New Jersey to the Tumble Inn? Would Fran still be alive? Would Nat even *be*? And what would Nat's life and mine have been like had she and I ended up moving to New Jersey instead of staying here when I'd refused to turn the key in the ignition and then tackled and literally held her to the ground on that day eight months ago? Would she have been happier? Would I? I suppose there would have been more, or different, opportunities down in New Jersey. More possible jobs, perhaps a brighter future for me, and perhaps a better school for Nat. Of course there would have been the proximity of my parents and Fran's, their help and stability. There would have been some old friends, like Howie. And maybe I'd have gotten to know Joanne better. There might have been opportunities that I can't imagine. But dangers, too. A very late transition to a new high school for Nat. Friends way faster and more sophisticated than she. The drugs and alcohol of affluent teenagers. Designer clothes. Fancy proms. The canned music, stale air, and mindless consumerism of suburban shopping malls. And that's to say nothing of the people here that we'd miss, and the lake, the mountain, the brook, the rise and fall of the hills. Like I said, how can you tell?

What I can tell you is what it's been like here over the last eight months. There was another period, including Nat's birthday, of resentful silence. She stayed in her room. For a short time, she pulled her hair again. Things were horrible, and yet almost imperceptibly, over a number of months, came our slow and fitful accommodation to our continuing lives here.

On the day that I tackled Nat, carried her back to the inn, and after she'd fallen asleep, I cancelled my appointments in New Jersey. I called my parents, Fran's, and Joanne to tell them we wouldn't be moving south anytime soon, or perhaps ever—about that I couldn't be sure. With varying expressions of surprise, they disapproved of, reluctantly acquiesced to, or, as in the case of Joanne, gracefully, if sadly, accepted our change of plans.

When I'd finally pressed all the buttons on the phone and Joanne came on the line, I couldn't get the words out straight.

"Are you trying to say you're not coming?" she asked.

"Yes."

No one spoke for a moment, until she said in her clear, deliberate voice, "Of course, I'm disappointed, but I understand. I really do. If we can, let's stay in touch."

"Okay," I said, though I think we both knew that it was unlikely. This felt like the tapering off of things, things that had never really had a chance to grow.

"Take care," she said in a way that let me know that she meant it.

"I will. You too."

Then on Nat's birthday, after I'd retrieved her boots from the woods, I did something that may have helped the two of us a little, though you wouldn't have known it at first. Because I couldn't think of any other present to give her, I began building a simple wooden raft that in the summer I could moor out on the lake beyond the dock, something for Nat to swim *to.* I got an easy, step-by-step plan off the internet, bought the lumber and hardware at Stephenson's, and almost every day through the end of February, I spent an hour working on the raft in the garage. I'd turn on the space heater. I'd saw a few two-by-six boards, or drill some holes, or bolt the frame and stringers together, or nail the deck planks into place. It was just something I did and kept doing, something pretty straightforward and predictable that I couldn't screw up in a major way. Each day I'd tell Nat how the project was going, and each day she didn't say anything, didn't seem to care or even hear me, until one Saturday about a week after President's Day, she came into the garage wearing those boots again, and holding a hammer she'd found in the basement. Her face looked neither resigned nor determined, neither particularly happy nor sad. She just kneeled beside me on the edge of the raft, took a few nails from the tin can on the floor, and still without a word, started nailing down some planks herself.

Meanwhile, after an awkward conversation in which the principal assured me that Jimmy Phelps wouldn't be a problem anymore, Nat had returned to school, albeit reluctantly. I'd hired a tutor, a retired instructor at Utica College, to help her catch up in her classes. On a dare from her trigonometry teacher, she took the SAT in early March, and a month later, she got her scores. While hardly stellar, they were good enough to give her a chance at some state colleges that offered rolling admissions and financial aid, and that weren't "too picky," as she said.

This surprised and buoyed her, and put her in a more aspiring crowd in school. I'd forgotten how kids, with the right turn of fortune, can make quantum leaps. "Eventually she'll pull herself together," Fran had often said, and perhaps that was happening now. Nat checked out websites and sent in her applications, and on an evening in early May when I was emptying the dishwasher, she raced down the stairs with a printed-out email letter from SUNY-Oneonta, like a holy document in her hand. She had her hair pulled back with a single elastic band, which made her look streamlined. You could see her neck, as long as Fran's, and the smooth, straight line of her jaw. Her eyes were huge and, shaking with excitement, she could barely speak. She showed me the letter. "I did it!"

"Wonderful!" Without thinking, I threw my arms around her, hugged her tight, and, though she didn't respond in kind, she didn't stiffen or push me off.

I meant that hug with all my heart, yet she must have detected something else in my embrace or in my voice, and I think in her own heart as well. Oneonta is a hundred miles from here, and that's just geographical distance. She'd be leaving this place and leaving me, her childhood and my day-to-day parenthood sliding more quickly away. When I'd released her, she put down the letter and—this, too, reminded me of Fran—she looked at me with clear, unswerving eyes and said, "We're going to be all right. Both of us."

Something in and between Nat and me was beginning to loosen up. From last fall's supply of apples, she made applesauce again, and little by little, I was doing more of my usual spring jobs, though not always in a timely fashion. I raked and carted away the mundungus on the beach. When the grass on the knoll was a half foot high, I got around to mowing it. I hired our next configuration of summer "help," and along with Mabel and Abby, who drove up from Johnstown to reorganize the kitchen, we madly prepared for the deluge of Regulars. In the evenings, I started listening to Yankee games. The same smooth announcer, the same ads for Fox Woods Resorts, nearly the same batting order and same relief pitchers: Nelson, Hitchcock, Rivera in the ninth. That litany brought a calm end to those hectic days.

Though I couldn't have fully recognized or had words for it then, Fran's death, which still surprised me at odd moments, was softening and, like my skid marks on Route 8, fading by the beginning of the summer. I was as much troubled now by the dimming of my memories of her as I was overwhelmed by her absence. Some things that once had driven me crazy became tolerable and mysteriously, if painfully, sustaining. Her recorded voice on the message machine. Her brush on her bureau. Her sweaters in her drawers. Her shirts on hangers, her smell dissipating, while the stains remained under the sleeves. They all said, *She was my wife. We lived here. Look, I'm not making this up.*

In mid-June I finally went into the boathouse, slid the slings under the guide-boat, and winched it out of the water. It looked like the deer that I sometimes see crumped along the edge of the highway, a side caved in with broken ribs, and leaking. But Bruce Wagoner helped me haul it up the hill and lift it gently into the bed of the pickup, and I drove it to LeBlec's, where, over a couple of weeks, the guys made it seaworthy again.

Then on the same day that Bruce and I slid the repaired guide-boat back in the water and secured it on lines in the boathouse, we carried the finished raft from the garage down to the lake and, with Styrofoam blocks strapped underneath, moored it with a chain and cinderblocks about fifty yards out there. Soon Nat in her swimsuit was doing laps between the dock and the raft. I'll never forget that. It was her first time in the lake since Fran's death, and she swam the side stroke at a measured, easy, careful pace, reaching out, pulling forward, pausing, and reaching out again, as if feeling her way through the water, feeling it anew and savoring the old pleasure it gave her.

So all things considered, last spring and summer were an improving time for us. In May, we'd had separate visits from Fran's parents and mine. They were all pleased for Nat, and, given her plans for college, their calls for us to move to New Jersey had simmered down. In late June, Nat graduated from high school and soon organized a small, five-afternoons-a-week summer swimming camp here for five- to seven-year-olds, which seemed to open her pores. She loved it. Banging through the porch door about five o'clock when her camp was done, she was excited and "famished," "dying for dinner," and chock full of stories about "my kids." And while crazy and tiring, it was good for me to have the inn packed again that July and most of August, with all the noise, activity, and all the immediate and urgent problems: the plugged toilets, dripping faucets, and pork chops served to vegetarians. Most were problems I could fix.

That's basically how the summer, last summer, went, though as we scrambled toward its end, there was also a mounting pressure or weight, a sense that Nat and I were coming to something momentous and yet so ordinary that we barely spoke of it. It was in the air. It was behind all our words. It was in our eyes when they'd meet and glance away. It was what I thought about when I did my chores or as I turned off my lamp at night. What would leaving be like for Nat? How would she react? Would she be happy? What would it be like for me?

The approach of all this seemed to slow the events of the summer, and some of those events, as I see them now, comprised a ritual, a series of acts in which we tried to prepare ourselves for Nat's departure. We made lists and, when I could get away from the inn, went bargain hunting in Albany. We got deals on a cell phone and a refurbished laptop. I bought her a pair of earrings and a down coat to replace her pea jacket. Fresh piles arose on her bedroom rug: one for clothes, one for school materials, one you might label "personal hygiene," and another I could only construe as "extremely miscellaneous."

Still, I wasn't ready for what I saw one evening in the final days of August, after I'd said goodnight to the few remaining guests and had gone up to the annex. Nat's light was off. Already she was in bed and fast asleep. I looked into her room which, in the pale light from her window, was positively neat and clean. The piles of stuff on her floor had disappeared. The do-dads on her desk were nicely arranged. The only thing out of place was that suitcase, zipped closed, ready to go, standing next to the radiator.

From the Tumble Inn, you can get to Oneonta in two or three different ways, each taking about two and a half hours. The most direct way is to follow Route 10 west for forty miles to a town called Poland, where you turn due south on Route 28. It's a less dramatic drive than Route 30, which leads southeast through Amsterdam. For starters, when you're heading west and south, the downhill slope is less precipitous than the route to the east. Still, it's a nice, winding drive through the forest, and when you come down into the Mohawk Valley at Herkimer, you know you're leaving the Adirondacks, that dome of granite that rose to the earth's surface ten thousand years ago and has refused to be worn away.

What you're coming into, as you continue south of the Mohawk River, is a gentler, more open and pliable land that was scooped by glaciers into long lakes and shoved into low, rolling hills. The hilltops are wooded, the valleys fenced and cultivated. This is the great belt of farmland across the middle of the state, and now, driving through warm afternoon sun, Nat and I saw tall silos, red barns with tin gambrel roofs, and tractors with pigeon-toed front tires sticking out of big swinging doors. We saw cows, staring, just their cuds going, in muddy yards and tan pastures. In the early spring, you can ride for miles on these roads behind a heaped manure spreader, or on a day like this one, you might follow all manner of balers, or weird machines with disks and tines, or rickety wagons shedding hay and dust so thick that you have to turn on your wipers.

That morning before our trip to take her to college, Nat and I had eaten in the kitchen. Meanwhile, in the dining room, Mabel served breakfast to the guests who'd all be gone by that afternoon, as summers end so early now because schools get started so early. Afterwards, Nat had walked out to the lake for a long, last swim. I came down to the dock and watched her doing the backstroke, straight out a couple hundred yards, her long arms turning like spokes in a wheel.

At one point, she saw me, stopped, and waved with both arms, showing off, treading water with just her feet. "The water, it's glorious!" she'd called. "You should come on out!"

I called back, no thanks. "I'm happy just watching you." Which was true. Such a pleasure to see her swim.

Eventually she swam back in, diving and surfacing along the way, floating on her back, kicking and somersaulting, almost as she did when she was a kid. But with the sun gleaming on her shoulders as she stepped through the shallow water and came up on the beach, as she swung her hair, gathered it on one side, and wrung it with her hands, as she adjusted the straps of her swimsuit, then bent to pick up her towel and wrapped it around herself like a skirt . . . she was a young woman now.

Then about a half hour later, after she'd dressed and while I was doing my mid-morning chores, emptying trash barrels outside the garage, Nat had come up to me with a strange, earnest look in her face. Even more strange was what she held in her hands: the baby blue box of Fran's ashes.

I was stunned. *What's going on? How did she know where to find that box? How did she know what was in it?*

"I have an idea," she said.

And the funny thing was, I had a sense of her idea, as if it was my own, as well. For her, it must have been some uncanny instinct for her own beginning, while for me . . . well, it just seemed right, especially as this was the day of Nat's leaving. I even thought that Fran would approve. Knowing her, she'd be amused.

"Okay," I said to Nat. "Let's do it."

So, with Nat carrying the box, we'd walked up the driveway and down the dirt road. We turned off, and I followed her through the field, where the blueberries had gone by and the tall grasses, stiff as straw, brushed our shins. We came to the edge of the woods and went in. There it was cooler, the air thick and sweet, the path springy with pine needles. The brook moved sluggishly, quietly, lingering and backtracking in pools, like it always does in late August. We didn't go far upstream. We stopped on the bank where we stood on a wide rock that was more or less horizontal.

Having gotten us here, Nat all at once lost courage. "How do we do this?"

"I don't know. I've never done anything like it."

"Here," she said. "You take it."

She put the box into my hands. It was heavy, and I removed the top. The ashes were in a plastic bag that might hold a loaf of bread. "Maybe we should take turns," I said.

"Okay."

I unsealed the bag. "Can you make your hands into a bowl?"

She did this hesitantly, and, tilting the bag, I poured about a cup's worth into her palms. There were tiny shards of whitish bone, but mostly the ashes were gray particles. Nat held them for a moment, looking at or *into* them, her face as still as a painting. While right there beside me, she seemed to be in a place that was all her own and where I couldn't help her. She let the ashes fall through her fingers and onto the water, where they drifted a moment on their way to the lake, then disappeared.

I gave her the bag, and she poured some ashes into my hands. They were dry but neither light nor heavy, and as I let them go, it seemed I could feel every shard and grain, some sharp, some sugary, some as soft and fine as flour.

We went back and forth like this, until the bag was empty. We washed our hands in the cold water. I folded the bag into the box and put on the top. Single file, we headed back along the path, and on the road we walked side by side, each of us with an arm around the other.

Now, on our way to Oneonta that afternoon, as I drove with Nat in the passenger seat, with her floppy purse at her feet and her suitcase in the bed of the pickup, I turned onto Route 205. We passed through tiny towns, each with a church, a bank, and houses that clung so close to the road that we could almost reach out and touch their front porches. Then we were out in the open fields again, swaying with the pitch of the road, wooden fences ticking by, and the hay-scented air washing through the cab. For long periods we were quiet, just watching the land unfurl, and once, outside a town called Mount Vision, Nat's eyes went heavy and closed, and her head rolled to the side, rocking slightly between the door and the top of her seat. She was wearing denim shorts, a T-shirt, and flip-flops, her usual summer outfit that tried to say, *I'm easygoing. I'm casual.* The wind blew long strands of her hair that streamed outside her window, and sometimes I could see the shorter, finer wisps behind her ear, where she wore one of her new earrings, a tiny gold pearl. At one point, her mouth opened slightly, the map fell from her hand, and I thought of her as an infant in those red pajamas with feet, that moment when all the tension would leave her body, she'd fall asleep, and Fran and I would stare at each other in relief and amazement. *Just look what we've gotten ourselves into!*

Then I remembered farther back. Fran and I were in our old Volkswagen van, having skipped out of teaching our afternoon classes at Garfield High. We were heading north through similar farmland, not knowing where our lives were going, though it felt good to be moving, to be leaving something behind and heading into something else, whatever it was.

And whatever it was turned out to be a lot of things, many of them good, many of them surprising, some of them happy beyond imagination, and some of them just as sad. *Funny how you stumble into things, like your life. An innkeeper? On a lake in the Adirondack Mountains? It still seems pretty unlikely. But that's where I've lived for twenty years. That's where I've worked. That's where I've had a wife who I've loved and lost. That's where I've had a daughter who I've loved with all the remains of my heart. . . .*

And now I'm taking her away.

If Fran were here, she might have made this part of the trip easier, the part when we were only ten miles from Oneonta, well beyond the point of turning back. Sitting on the passenger side with Nat squeezed between us, she might have reeled off a few knock-knock jokes or gotten us to play I-spy

She'd certainly have had some choice things to say about my driving: *How in the world, when you're going so slowly, can you manage to run a stop sign?* Or: *Look at that farm stand! Bushels of apples! Stop. Pull over. Next week I'll make pies. We'll need some cheering up!* Or maybe she'd have come right out and said to Nat what was on her mind and on mine at the moment: *You know, it seems like yesterday when you were an infant, asleep on my shoulder.* And Nat would say, *Mom, you're getting all gushy.* Then after a while, Fran would reply, breaking the mood and making us smile, *You're right. As a baby, you were a pain in the ass!*

But most importantly, on our way home after leaving Nat at college, Fran would still be there beside the passenger window. She'd be quiet, gazing at the road ahead, and perhaps she'd turn on the radio and find a country music station to fill up the space between us. Nat's leaving would have been Fran's loss as much as mine, or probably even more than mine. In any case, we would have shared it.

"Dad, you all right?" Nat had come awake and was sitting up straight. Without knowing it, I'd taken my foot off the gas, and we were slowing down, passing some rusted, crammed-together mailboxes near the end of a dirt lane. "Do you want me to drive?" I could feel her staring at the side of my face.

"I'm okay." I pushed the gas and we gathered speed. To show her that I really *was* okay, I asked her about the classes she wanted to take, though I knew what they were already. I told her how I thought that she'd have a great year at college, that she was at an exciting time, when she'd meet all kinds of people, and she'd be learning so many things, things that I hadn't even heard of. Her life, I said, would be widening and deepening, and she'd be discovering new and wonderful capacities in herself. I told her how proud I was of her and how I admired her, because she'd survived the worst thing that I could imagine and was stepping out into the world. Who knew where her life might take her?

Even though she wasn't sleepy now, Nat got quiet again, the way she often did when I tried to be serious, when I was getting "too parental," as she'd say. She looked away and out her window, lost in her thoughts.

Soon we were going down a steep hill, the road wavering in the afternoon heat. Some ramshackle houses bunched up on one side, some disused industrial buildings on the other. We passed a Dairy Queen. A cell phone tower rose in the distance.

"Looks like we're about there," I said.

20

As campuses go, the SUNY College at Oneonta is not picturesque, though the hills around it are. Most of the buildings are brick and boxy in that institutional 1970's style, and Tobey Hall, Nat's dormitory, is no exception. It has two identical wings, each with a flat roof, flat sides, and three layers of windows, eight across, all lined up in a grid. Slowing down around a long turn, we headed for the lot immediately in front, where other parents had parked. Cars and shiny SUVs—not another pickup in sight—seemed to have exploded with packed-in stuff from open trunks, doors, and hatches. Kids lugged armloads toward the dorm: computers, printers, houseplants, coffee makers, pillows, lamps, and tennis rackets. Someone, I recall, carried a crate of oranges, someone else a goldfish swaying in a bowl, and someone else pushed an entire garment rack on clattering wheels. For the most part, the boys wore baggy shorts and T-shirts. A few seemed impossibly tall. A few had gelled hair. Others, with scruffy beards, threw footballs back and forth, while others walked about, talking importantly, a cell phone clammed on an ear. Some girls wore tube tops that showed off their breasts and tan stomachs. Others sported polo shirts and boat shoes. Already music was pumping out dorm windows, making everything vibrate. With a pang, I wondered how Nat could fit in here, and I imagined she was wondering the same thing.

All this time, she'd been quiet, her face turned away toward the passenger side window, as if the landscape was still flying by. When I'd parked, I reached over and put my hand on her shoulder, which was tight as a knot. "Don't worry," I said, though I was worrying myself. "You'll be fine here."

In about an hour, at 5:00, there would be a "students only" barbeque followed by an orientation meeting, so we had time to get Nat's things up to her room before I'd have to leave. I got out and walked around to her door. Her face was solemn, and it seemed like both the face of a child and that of someone who'd already been through college and was wondering what to do next with her life.

"How about if I grab your bag?" I said.

She nodded. Then I opened her door and she stepped out. Something about her bare feet, her thin toes in her flip-flops, gave me another pang.

I slid her suitcase out of the back. I tried to be funny and jolly her along. "Shall we go in and check the place out? I wonder what their rates are?"

She gave me her mildly exasperated look, which meant she was wise to what I was doing.

"Let's go find your room," I said more directly.

I took the suitcase, she put her purse over her shoulder, and together we crossed the parking lot and the sidewalk where, hanging from the edge of a striped tent, a sign said, "Welcome, Class of 2009!" Behind a table, cheery sophomores, who called themselves VIPs, welcomed Nat like a long lost sister. They asked her to initial some papers on a clipboard, then gave her a key and a printed self-adhesive tag with a smiley face ("Hello! My name is Natalie Finley!"), like the ones that other freshmen had slapped on the fronts of their T-shirts. Nat held hers in her hand.

I followed her through a crowded lobby, up three flights of stairs—the first and third floors were for girls—and down a long hallway. Her purse, though not nearly so heavy as the suitcase I lugged, made her shoulders bend to the right, and as we neared her room, passing #309, #311, and #313 on the left, she moved more slowly, her flip-flops barely clicking on her heels.

#315 was about what you'd expect of a standard double room in Tobey Hall. The words "small," "spare," and "symmetrical" pretty much cover it. An oatmeal-colored vinyl floor. Along one wall, a battered pine desk, a pine chair, and a pine-framed bed. A matching set lined the opposite wall, and two identical pine dressers were centered beneath a window. It all smelled faintly of Lysol.

I seem to remember every detail of the place, but I couldn't have taken them all in right then, for when we went through the door, we immediately met Nat's roommate and parents. The five of us plus luggage filled the room. We could barely move around. We all shook hands.

The roommate was Megan, an Irish name, though with her tanned arms and legs and long, blonde hair, she didn't look too Irish to me. She had that proud, muscled look of an athlete, a look I still can't get used to on girls. She wore yellow gym shorts and a jersey with intersecting lacrosse sticks on the front. Her dad, in tasseled loafers, a sport coat, and open collar, exuded a casual air, as though he wouldn't be much put out by the tuition or the room and board here. He was friendly and outgoing, and for some reason, I can't recall much about Megan's mother, except for a small, monogrammed canvas bag that hung from the crook of her arm.

We made small talk. They were from White Plains, a Westchester suburb north of New York City, and Megan was indeed a lacrosse player, the captain of her high school team. She also allowed that she was good at acting, and had been the lead in her school musicals three years in a row. She said she might be a double major in psychology and theater arts. There didn't seem to be anything she couldn't do.

Soon she and her parents excused themselves. They all wanted to take a walk before her folks would head home. We shook hands again, and they went out, leaving the door half-closed behind them.

Since Megan's many bags, along with a microwave and a mini-refrigerator, covered the bed to the left, we put Nat's suitcase on the other bed, and I sat beside it. That's when I really looked around and took in the whole room. Meanwhile, Nat sat on the adjacent desk chair, bent forward, her elbows on her knees, and stared at her hands, where she curled the name tag around her index finger, then rolled it between her palms. She still had her purse on her shoulder.

I said, "As soon you get some books in here, and maybe a rug and posters on the walls, you'll start feeling at home."

Nat didn't say anything. Some girls, laughing, passed outside the door.

"In fact, I think we have some extra throw rugs in the attic," I went on. "I could bring you one next weekend."

Still, she didn't say anything. She took a long breath and finally said very evenly, "But you know, that really isn't the problem."

"What is?"

She stopped rolling the name tag and put it on the desk. She rubbed her palms on her shorts. She turned her head and looked right at me. "Dad," she said. "I can't."

"Can't what?" I asked, though I knew what she'd meant.

"I can't stay here. I'm coming home with you." She said this in that assured tone that Fran always used when she'd made up her mind and there was no changing it back. But there was something else in Nat's voice that wouldn't have been in Fran's. It was something only between Nat and me. It was all we'd lived through, daughter and father—all the sobbing, the listlessness, the rage, the blood, the pulled hair, the slammed doors, the brooding silences, the glimmers of joy, the grief and love—all of it. And it was also in her eyes, which were welling up, for me it seemed. She didn't look away.

"No," I said after a while. "You can't come home. Don't worry about me. I'm fine. Why don't we unpack a few things?" I reached over, put my hand on her shoulder again, and I could still feel that tightness.

"I'm coming home," she repeated in that same voice.

"But what about all those courses you'll be taking? The friends you'll make? You're feeling exactly what you should be feeling now. Every other kid here is nervous and scared, even—what's her name?—Megan."

"There's a difference," Nat said.

For an instant, we just looked at each other, and of course I understood: Megan had been standing with *both* her parents.

"I'm coming home," Nat said again.

Some more kids walked past the door. Music, though muted, pulsed through the floor and walls. Beyond the window, I could see rows of yellowing corn stalks on the low hills south of town. Back home at the inn, the first leaves were turning yellow at the top of the mountain, and the lake would be smooth as glass. The beach quiet. The parking lot empty. The swings still. The grass tan. The summer done, and no one else around. If we were there right then, I'd have finished picking up things that guests had left on the beach and in the boathouse: a kid's plastic pail, ruffled paperbacks, a couple of T-shirts, a sandal. I'd have gone up to the porch where Nat might have hung quilts to air out over the railings, that scent of mothballs on the breeze. Maybe she'd be reading in a rocker or watering the potted plants beside the door, and we'd chat about what we'd make for dinner.

"Look," I said at last. "Let's make a deal. Try staying here for just this week, that's all. I think you'll like it, but if you don't, I'll drive down next weekend and bring you home. I promise. All right?"

She shook her head, no, and looked at the floor, tears running down her face. Like Fran, she was never what you'd call "beautiful." There's always been that narrowness about her, and her narrowness is altogether different from Fran's, less sharp and assertive, more fragile and fleeting. Often I've had the sense that if Nat turned a certain way, she might actually disappear. But sitting there in that room, my thin-hipped, motherless daughter—she was beautiful beyond words to me.

"Are you sure that's what you want to do?" I asked. "Leave now and go home?"

"Yes. I'm sure."

For a few more moments, we didn't or couldn't speak. How much sense did this make? Just seven months after I'd forced her to stay home, I was pleading with her to stay away.

In part because we'd been on the road for over two hours and I've reached the age when certain events come more frequently, but mostly because I didn't know what else to do, I said, "I need to use the rest room."

"It's on the second floor." And smiling through her tears, Nat added, "Don't worry. That one's just for guys."

"I'll be right back." I went out the door and closed it to give her some privacy. I walked down the hall and a flight of stairs toward the boys' floor. Some party was already in full swing at 4:45 on a Monday afternoon, and I thought I heard beer bottles clinking over the throbbing music.

As you might guess, the rest room on that floor already had a certain aroma that encouraged you to get on with your business. I came out, thinking, *What would Fran do in this situation? Bring Nat home? Or somehow make her stay? How?* But then if Fran *was* here, the situation, as Nat had pointed out, would have been different. Nothing would be the same. I had no idea what Fran might have said or done.

I went back up the stairs and down the hall toward #315. As I got near, I saw that the door was part-way open again, and I heard conversation inside. Megan had come back—her parents had gone home—and she and Nat were alone. Before I turned into the room, I stopped, leaned against the wall where they couldn't see me, and listened. Megan, of course, was doing most of the talking, though I wouldn't say she was holding forth as before. She reported that there were long lines at the bookstore. She said she'd met the Resident Advisor who was "nice." Then Nat asked Megan when her birthday was, and Megan said it was in April. Now they were quiet, painfully so, a couple of kids haphazardly thrown together, grasping awkwardly for anything to talk about.

After a moment, Megan said, "You know, already I miss my friends from home."

"Yeah," Nat agreed, though without much spark in her voice.

Then Megan said, "This room. I mean, it's pretty grim. Isn't it?"

Again Nat just said, "Yeah."

"So what do you think we should do about it?"

And to my surprise, Nat replied, "It'll need a rug and some posters on the walls."

"What colors do you like?"

"Tans and yellows. Warm colors."

"Same with me," Megan said.

Soon Nat asked Megan what she'd been doing that summer, and Megan described a number of sports camps she'd attended. Some of them were okay, she said, but in others "they push you too hard, like sports are your whole life. How about you?"

"I ran a camp for little kids," Nat said, her voice more energetic. "I live on a lake up north."

"No kidding!"

Then Nat actually told Megan how she had organized the camp, had signed up the children, and every weekday from 9:00 to noon, had led or supervised their activities. Then she spoke about a number of her campers in particular, about how, one by one and hand in hand, she'd walk them, shivering, out into the water, up to their knees, to their waists, and to their chests, how she'd show them how to blow bubbles, how to cup their hands, to rotate their arms with their elbows high, and to reach way out, as far as they could, and pull the lake toward them. She told Megan how she'd get the kids to float by holding her arms under their legs and stomachs, and how they'd thrash, kick, and paddle like crazy, and then maybe, eventually, swim.

"That's wonderful!" Megan said. "I wish I could've done something like that!"

They were quiet again, but this was a different kind of quiet, like a pause to absorb what they'd been saying.

All at once, as though taken unawares, Nat said, "My dad! I wonder what's happened to him!"

And that's when I did it. A pure reflex, and then something more. I turned and started moving away, retracing my steps. Of course, I'd promised Nat I'd never leave her. And I'd meant it. I'm the only parent she's got left, and she's my only child.

But this, it seemed, was how it had to happen, if it ever was to happen at all. To have gone back in that room, for our eyes to have met, to have seen everything about her that reminds me of Fran, and for her to have seen me again for what I am—an innkeeper, a widower, a father who's a little less needed each day—I don't know what we'd have done. Or not done.

So I kept moving. Like I've said, it's the most ordinary and natural thing, a kid leaving home, and it's not at all like when someone you love dies. It's not absolute, not irrevocable. Still, it can turn you inside out. I walked down the hall, past knots of chattering students. I walked down the stairs to the first floor, my hand gripping the railing. I kept walking through the lobby, across the sidewalk and the parking lot, where I could smell hamburgers grilling. I got into the pickup and started the engine. I backed out of the parking space and steered toward the exit. I didn't turn my eyes from the road. I shifted into first and let out the clutch. I hit the gas and, with all that was in me, held my foot down.

I decided to go back to the inn by the eastern route, even though it's some miles longer. I took Interstate 88 to Schoharie, where I stopped for gas. I went north on Route 30 through Amsterdam and along the west shore of Sacandaga Lake. Then, at the bridge above Northville, I crossed to the east side of the river. Maybe there are a few more cottages along the road since Fran and I had driven up here nineteen years ago, and surely there are more satellite dishes in the yards, but mainly it all looks the same. First came the foothills, the birch, beech, and maple trees. Then beyond Wells the houses petered out. The road climbed through hardwoods mixed with pine-scented spruce, hemlock, and fir. And then, far ahead, the mountains rose in familiar, dark green waves, the sun splashed on their western flanks.

When I was back at the inn, I phoned Nat to check in and say I was home safely. She said that she and Megan had just returned to their room from the orientation meeting, and some girls from down the hall had dropped by. I was surprised by how pleased she sounded. I could hear laughter in the background. I asked her how things were going. "Fine," she said, and then the laughter seemed to recede, as if, with her phone, she'd stepped out into the hall. In a quieter tone, she said, "Dad, you didn't even say goodbye." It was more a statement of fact than an accusation.

"I know. I'm sorry. But I couldn't do it any other way."

"It's okay," she said.

I could tell that she wanted to get back to the conversation in her room, so I said, "Let's talk soon."

"Yes. Thanks for calling."

We said goodnight and rang off.

Now it's almost two months later. I haven't seen Nat since I left her in Oneonta, though we talk on the phone on Sunday evenings, and in another month or so—thirty-one days, to be precise—I'll drive down there again, pick her up, and we'll head to New Jersey for Thanksgiving, which we'll spend with Fran's parents and mine. From what I can gather, and while you can never know how long anything will last, she seems happy and busy. She got into most of the classes she wanted. She and Megan are getting along. Together they study in some place they call "the dungeon," and on Saturdays, they go into town for pizza. As it turns out, they found an old braided rug for their room at a flea market, and I imagine it's now covered with books, iPods, clothes, crumbs, damp towels, coffee stains, cell phones, and who-knows-what. A ratty rug in a regular college dorm room.

In our conversations, Nat hasn't said anything about wanting to come home, say, for some weekend before Thanksgiving. Nor have we said anything more about that day when I left her. I don't know how she found out that I'd gone, if she eventually went out of her dorm room, down the hall, downstairs, out on the sidewalk, and searched for the pickup in the parking lot. I don't know what her face looked like at that moment, or how stunned and abandoned she might have felt. Or maybe—I hope—she might have already understood that one way or another we'd have to tear ourselves apart, that pain is often the measure of love, and maybe her mind, if not relieved, was made more clear: she was beginning the next part of her life.

As for me, I think I'm also doing all right, though things feel different without Nat around and without my even knowing how she's doing from day to day. I still have moments that take my breath away and for a while leave me in a state of wonder and weakness, when I'm not much good for anything. Usually they come on weekday late-afternoons, after Mabel has put in a few hours work, when no one else is here, and the sun falls earlier and earlier behind the hills. I find myself listening for the smack of the porch door when Nat would come in from her swimming camp, kicking off sneakers, dropping her backpack in a heap, and calling, "I'm famished! What's for dinner?" That's when I wonder who she's eating with now. *Is she ever lonely? Is she ever homesick? Does she have days when she just wants to hide away?*

And sometimes on those late weekday afternoons when I watch the sun go down, I think of Fran, our fights, our laughter and tears, and then I feel in my hands the curve of her back, the smooth dent at the base of her spine, and against my thigh the press of her hip, as we'd stand on the porch or out on the knoll, looking at these same hills.

Still, on weekends, I'm revived and amused by the Leaf Peepers and bird-watchers who totter in from their hikes, loaded down with binoculars, cameras, notebooks, and field guides like the Christmas presents I'd received from Nat, one of which I always keep in my pocket. On weekday mornings, I get up with the clamoring grosbeaks and blue jays, those stubborn and obstreperous birds that, like me, don't fly south for the winter. I set a fire and get it going. After breakfast, I drive to Orma's for coffee and my daily fill of bad jokes and wry commentary. Sometimes I contribute my own. At the market in Speculator, I grab a newspaper and a few groceries. I stop for lumber or hardware at Stephenson's, where the talk is of football and "big bucks," by which they don't mean lots of cash—it's deer season. Often on my way home, I'll pass Jim Owen driving in the opposite direction, his cruiser swirling up leaves behind him, the only car for miles. It's like that up here during the fall. People are few and far between, but they'll come quick if you need them. As we pass, Jim and I wave the way Year-Rounders do, just lifting a few fingers off the wheel, which means *See you around.*

Then, by mid-morning, when the caffeine is really cranking and the sun has melted the frost on the knoll, I'll finally get down to work. I've already hauled the swimming raft ashore, put it on cinderblocks, and covered it with the tarp until next summer. I've stowed the canoes upside down on their racks in the boathouse. I've winched the guide-boat out of the water and brushed on another coat of varnish. I've hung and hooked in all the storm windows. So mostly now it's raking leaves, splitting wood, repairing the dock, and, for a couple hours each day, I've been putting together some income-and-expense numbers for the board meeting next week. In the evenings, I talk now and then with Fran's parents or mine, and sometimes the Wagoners come over to play cards. Most nights, I eat dinner with the radio on, and—can you believe it?—the White Sox are in the World Series. This, after the Red Sox won it all last year. Something strange is going on.

As I've said, Fran thought that you can always change your life, go somewhere else, do something different, begin all over. She may very well have been right about that, and at some point my life could change again. I might do something altogether different. I might not be an innkeeper. As Nat grows up and cuts her own path, I might move away from here. In a corner of my mind, I can imagine that sometime, somewhere, say when I'm shopping down in Albany or visiting in New Jersey, I might run into someone else. I might look up Joanne or some other acquaintance, one thing could lead to another, and I might eventually remarry and live in a surprising way that bears little resemblance to my life with Fran and my life right now.

But for a while, at least, I think I'll stay put. This still feels right to me. For your life, like a brook, can flow into, spread out, deepen, and accumulate in a place, and eventually that place, its people that you've known, put up with, or loved, and all you've done and all that's happened there . . . well, you can't just get up one fine morning and walk away from it. Instead of leaving it, I'd rather live in the place where my life has been, where I've become who I am. I'd rather let it seep in and fill my heart to overflowing, before I move on, if I do, to another place.